SOMEWHERE NORTH OF NORMAL

STORIES

Adam Lindsay Honsinger

ENFIELD & WIZENTY

Enfield & Wizenty
(an imprint of Great Plains Publications)
1173 Wolseley Avenue
Winnipeg, MB R3G 1H1
www.greatplains.mb.ca

Great Plains Publications gratefully acknowledges the financial support provided for
its publishing program by the Government of Canada through the Canada Book
Fund; the Canada Council for the Arts; the Province of Manitoba through the Book
Publishing Tax Credit and the Book Publisher Marketing Assistance Program; and
the Manitoba Arts Council.

Design & Typography by Relish New Brand Experience
Bird imagery by Adam Lindsay Honsinger
Printed in Canada by Friesens

LIBRARY AND ARCHIVES CANADA CATALOGUING IN PUBLICATION

Honsinger, Adam Lindsay, 1963-, author
        Somewhere north of normal : stories / Adam Lindsay Honsinger.

Issued in print and electronic formats.
ISBN 978-1-77337-006-4 (softcover).--ISBN 978-1-77337-007-1 (EPUB).--
ISBN 978-1-77337-008-8 (Kindle)

    I. Title.

PS8615.O505S66 2018   C813'.6   C2018-904155-2
                                       C2018-904156-0

ENVIRONMENTAL BENEFITS STATEMENT

Great Plains Publications saved the following
resources by printing the pages of this book on
chlorine free paper made with 100% post-consumer
waste.

TREES	WATER	ENERGY	SOLID WASTE	GREENHOUSE GASES
2	180	1	8	962
FULLY GROWN	GALLONS	MILLION BTUs	POUNDS	POUNDS

Environmental impact estimates were made using the Environmental Paper Network
Paper Calculator 4.0. For more information visit www.papercalculator.org.

Canadä

FSC
www.fsc.org
MIX
Paper from
responsible sources
FSC® C016245

CONTENTS

This book is dedicated to my brothers, Chris, Greg, Grant, and Jeff.

FOREWORD

Some years ago on a Sunday afternoon stroll I encountered an ordinary eight-and-a-half-by-eleven-inch handwritten notice taped to a lamppost. It was entitled *An Open Love Letter*, and in a barely legible paragraph it professed an appreciation for such things as peeling paint, light, rust, and decay. Below the paragraph, the anonymous author had drawn a map of the neighbourhood onto which twelve specific locations were marked with an x, each of which promised to reward the viewer with an example of the sadness and beauty inherent all around us if one took the time to stop and look.

The first x on the map was only half a block away, so I carefully removed the notice from the lamppost and headed down the street. When I got to the place indicated on the map, I found chalked onto the pavement a circle with an eye in its centre and an arrow which pointed at the wall of an abandoned warehouse. The brick had long ago been painted a vibrant blue and was now chipped and peeling. I noticed after some contemplation that the original reddish colour of the exposed brick formed the shape of a near-perfect heart. It was indeed a pleasing and curious example of naturally occurring art set against the ravishing forces of neglect and decay, which of course satisfied the promise of the notice's thesis.

The next location required a more focussed degree of attention and patience. Standing in front of an old, second-hand bookstore, I found myself once again searching for something exceptional that might warrant this location's inclusion on the map. It was a cloudless October afternoon and, after several minutes gazing into the window, it struck me that the intention might be to simply stop and appreciate the pleasant way the sun illuminated the covers of the books on display. As I scanned the titles (most of which were classics), I was reminded of how brick-and-mortar bookstores like this one were slowly becoming a thing of the past. It was at that moment that the glass I was looking through became a divide between two dimensions of time, and the longer I stared at the dusty covers on the other side, I began to see those books as artefacts, something representational as opposed to useful or otherwise in current demand—sad and beautiful, indeed.

As I continued to follow the map, I was introduced to several more unique settings, all of which further conspired to affect my state of mind. Some destinations revealed nothing more than an angle of light falling on a keyhole or a fire hydrant gleaming yellow in the sun, but this exercise of taking the time to scrutinize and contemplate the things I strolled by each and every day had turned my neighbourhood into a curated gallery of perception.

The last marked symbol was located, to my astonishment, across the street from the old, dilapidated house in which I rented an attic apartment. I scanned the property for any irregularities, but aside from the fact that the rusted eaves over the porch were hanging a little lower than I remembered, I couldn't detect anything particularly unusual. The clue, I discovered, was written on the notice itself. Barely legible next to this final location, the mapmaker had written: 5:49 a.m., *third floor, window on the left.* The window I was being directed to was that of my apartment's kitchen. Though I had spent a considerable amount of time looking out this window, I had rarely looked in. I squinted my eyes, tilted my head to the left and the right, and while I still couldn't discern anything noteworthy, I began to feel as if I had entered an altered state of lucidity—awake in a dream—a sleepwalker—conscious in a subconscious place. My breath, which I could now see every time I exhaled, alerted me to the fact that the sun was setting and that I was indeed awake.

As I made my way up the staircase to my apartment, I found myself thinking of the writer Jorge Louis Borges and two of his stories,

"The Zahir" and "The Aleph," both of which are accounts of the author's forays into altered realities where, like in a dream, the impossible becomes real. In both stories, the narrators' epiphanies were inspired by an external symbol. In the case of "The Zahir," this symbol was a simple coin that, in the writer's possession, revealed its previous incarnations as a Persian astrolabe sunk in the Mediterranean Sea, a compass wrapped in a turban, a vein running through a marble column in Tetuan. This coin haunted Borges to the point of obsession, revealing subtle and fleeting glimpses of its metaphoric power. The Aleph materialized in a friend's basement staircase. It could be viewed only by lying down on the floor and fixing one's gaze on the nineteenth step. In one long paragraph spanning pages 150-151 in Borges's *Personal Anthology*, we learn that the Aleph is when all things in the world exist at once and are experienced from every possible angle, the micro- and the macrocosm, the Shangri-La of alchemists, Kabbalists, and magicians.

Like the Aleph and the Zahir, the symbol of the eye in the circle took root in my consciousness and I spent the evening with my head full of metaphysical ponderings. The symbol appeared everywhere I looked. I saw it at the bottom of my cup of tea, in the reflection in the window, in the television screen, on the insides of my eyelids. I couldn't stop noticing details that I had never seen before. Everything that I looked at revealed itself as a thing of exceptional originality. Even the darkness as I slowly drifted into sleep seemed to contain meaning and possibility, hope, mystery, and wonder.

I awoke to my alarm at 5:30 a.m.—the time I always arise on weekday mornings—and stumbled into the kitchen. Still half-asleep, I groggily performed my morning routine: pulling open the cutlery drawer, taking the milk out of the fridge, dropping slices of bread into the toaster. I had just finished loading and turning on the coffeemaker when I remembered the notice. I threw on some clothes, stumbled down the stairs, crossed the empty street and stood in the chalk circle. My bare feet were cold against the morning cement as I fixed my eyes on the curtains of my kitchen window. I anticipated the rising sun playing some trick of light on the glass, but it was still dark and as such, the potential for anything illuminating appeared unlikely. I counted down the last seven seconds on my watch until, at precisely 5:49, the curtains were drawn and, as I raised a cup of coffee to my lips and stared down at the street, our eyes met. I inhaled sharply and dropped the mug I was holding, which shattered in the circle with the eye in its centre drawn on my kitchen floor.

Borges' response to what can be described as two otherworldly experiences was to document them—his familiarity with metaphor and narrative allowed him to convert the impossible into the language of story. Where fact and fiction meet, we enter the dream, a place where the less stable elements of reality may bend, swaths of time may be leapt through in a single paragraph. It is here that the creative process may be mapped in a journey that traverses thousands of miles and goes back in time, a dying butterfly may inspire a revelation, an artist's body may become a work of art after being electrocuted, a man may wake up after falling four stories to find himself face-to-face with his fourteen-year-old self. This bridging of rationality, of time and space, this willingness to flirt with and, in some cases, outright defy that which we hold to be impossible is rooted to varying degrees in each story of this collection, not simply because fiction allows it, but because it is within the geography of the imagination that the lost souls of this collection attain transcendence, metamorphosis, and emotional reconciliation.

—*Adam Lindsay Honsinger*

FLOTSAM AND JETSAM

Aside from a table, a chair, and a few books of poetry, my office is otherwise empty. The walls are white, the curtains are drawn, there is no Internet connection. It is a monk's chamber. No distractions. None except the excruciating pain centred in my lower back.

I often suffer a degree of discomfort when struggling to work my long-winded ideas within the corral of a rhyming couplet, but this pain is different. It doesn't feel like the ache of restriction, the rigours of form or meter; it feels more like gravity, like a weight pushing down on my spine, something that could only be described by metaphor.

My chiropractor blames the chair, the height of my desk—the ergonomics of my computer dependency, an assessment that does not take into consideration the forces at work in the internal notebooks of the writer. I suspect that this present distress is a manifestation of a gestating story—the weight of my imagination.

This morning, the pain was so bad that I could barely get out of bed. The simple act of preparing breakfast was a precarious affair as one hand was tasked with holding myself up, while the other reached into cupboards, poured coffee, and managed the lid of a childproof bottle of painkillers. I eventually made it to my office where I presently sit, determined to get to the bottom of this troubling paroxysm.

I have no choice but to trust the process. And so it begins with the unrestrained thoughts in my head—a description of my office, a diagnosis of the pain in my back, a first-person narrative. A page and a half in and the unformed shape of two characters emerge: the first is archetypal and familiar, he too is a little confused, but he is a celebrity of sorts and therefore more comfortable with odd and unexpected encounters; the second, just as vague, is representational, but solid, like something carved from a hunk of wood. I get a whiff of sea air, pungent and briny. And as I stumble through this precursive exercise, I enter the story.

On September 18, 1973, five days before Pablo Neruda died, I find myself at the door of his home in Isla Negra on the front porch, disoriented and exhausted, uncertain of how I got here, and just as importantly, why I am here. While it is easy to imagine the crash of the distant surf and the bite of salt in the air, what I know of his home is limited to a photo I had once seen depicting inscriptions carved by grieving fans into the fence in the front of this house. The roof was orange tin, the walls were painted grey, the door was red. The colour and texture of this photo gives the house a dimension and character that inspires me to proceed. I knock on Neruda's red wooden door and I hear the distant sound of my fingers tapping away at the keyboard, which confirms that I am somewhere in between, still groping for purchase and purpose. As I wait for an answer, the pain in my back has me reaching for the railing that is, like the rest of the house, still so vague that I am surprised and relieved to find that it holds my weight. It's during this reprieve that I decide to take stock of what I know of Neruda—he was/is an icon, a poet, and a politician. His Hitchcockian face as big and as round as the ocean, he was a romantic who wrote with equal passion about chestnuts, mermaids, and love. He was a turner of stones, a boat rocker, a materialist, a collector of flotsam and jetsam.

When the door opens, he is wearing an undershirt and a pair of purple satin boxers. On his face, he is wearing the look of a man who has just awoken from a deep sleep. I extend my hand, but he hesitates and takes a moment to look me up and down as if I am a spectre from a dream. He eventually smiles and, as we shake hands, I am struck by a sudden and absurd image—dandelions gone to seed next to a glass of finely aged wine. I then flip open my Spanish dictionary, but the ocean breeze makes it difficult to manage the pages.

"*Como esta ud? Estoy admirer, a tourista...*" I turn the pages, frantically looking for the last word. Pablo picks up a white cat that has appeared at his feet. He seems pleasantly amused by both my struggles with the dictionary and the cat's playful antics in his arms. The moment I find the word I'm looking for, Neruda lets the cat drop to the floor and, before I can speak, he whispers, "*Ficcion,*" the utterance of which transports me suddenly and without ceremony back to my apartment in East Vancouver.

The first thing I notice is that along with the stress in my back, my feet are now tender and bruised as well. I begin to wonder if these discomforts might be the result of something I may have been carrying—something heavy and cumbersome—something that I might have hauled a long way. I slowly hobble out to the living room, grab an atlas from the bookshelf, and run a finger along the coast from Vancouver to Chile. Seven lines of latitude, the equator, the Tropic of Capricorn—approximately 5,456 miles.

I place the atlas back on the shelf, locate my copy of Neruda's *The Captain's Verses*, and look for clues. The poems are chaptered into themes of *love, desire, the furies, and lives*—broken lines forming long columns of text. The poems are simple and lucid and yet each one gives me pause. Each subject, be it the earth, an insect, or a dream, is spoken to, venerated, and illuminated in the poet's gaze. While sifting through a piece called "El Sueno," I'm distracted by the sound of someone or something knocking things about down the hall. After determining that the disturbance is located in the bathroom, I discover that a heavy wind coming in from the open window over the tub has toppled a can of shaving foam and a bottle of conditioner. I pull the windows closed and then pause at the sink to splash water on my face. The sound of the water and the invigorating effect it has on my skin reminds me of the words I had moments ago read—

and I, sinking and coming out, decided that you should come out of me, that you were weighing me down...[1]

And as I glance at my reflection in the mirror, I see her peering back at me over my shoulder—a weather-beaten, carved oak, ship's figurehead.

I came across her six months ago in a run-down shop on Hastings Street. I was poking about in a pile of rusted winches, busted sextants, compasses, and other nautical scrap when the perfect roundness of her breasts caught my eye. She was wind worn, slightly waterlogged, and smelled of seaweed and motor oil. When I freed her from the tangle of junk, I heard what sounded like a long breath of relief being exhaled from her blue lips. I paid the shopkeeper, lugged her home, brought her to the bathroom where, after a good cleaning, she has remained propped up against the wall ever since.

As I stare at her reflection in the mirror, it dawns on me that she is the missing element I have been searching for: she is the reason my back hurts, she is the reason my feet are sore. Her face, though somewhat worse for wear, still bears a countenance of will and purpose. It's not hard to imagine what she would say if she could in fact speak—*Take me to Pablo Neruda.*

I make haste back to my computer and start a new paragraph.

■

I am so inspired by the figurehead that the absurdity of this idea doesn't give me a moment's pause. I strap her securely to my back, grab my laptop, the book of Neruda's poems, and ride the Skytrain to Surrey, catch a bus to White Rock, and start walking south. It is on this leg of what I am sure will be a long and arduous journey that she does indeed start to talk. Mostly it sounds like gibberish, words like *spun yarn*, *scuttled butt*, and *marline spikes*, the meaning of which I can only guess at. Her voice is high and airy at first, but as she continues to mutter incoherently the timbre and tone lowers a little and becomes more breathy and sure.

After a six-hour hike along Highway 5, I smuggle her into the men's dorm of a hostel in Bellingham, WA where I tuck her in beside me and kiss her gently on the forehead goodnight. While lying in that darkness, her nonsensical nattering becomes less urgent, more meditative and clear, to the point that I recognize what sounds like a series of nautical directions. As I drift into sleep, I find myself imagining the swell and fall of the sea, a favourable wind, the unknowable horizon.

In the morning, I use the hostel's wifi to further my understanding of the man I am journeying towards. I read that Neruda was a collector. His house was full of clocks, sextants, astrolabes, hats, ships in bottles, French postcards, and of course ship's figureheads. His penchant for surrounding himself with things that he loved also included his beloved Chile and his third wife, Matilde Urrutia, whom he married twice. I imagine her as a curator to a living museum, taking care of a man whose lifetime she knew would be a fraction of the legacy of his fame. I read about his political views, his escape into exile under the pseudonym Antonio Ruiz, his trips to Europe and his soirees with eminent and curious company—Miguel Hernandez, García Lorca, and Eduardo Galeano. The passion he innately felt for the simplest of things was most famously expressed in his odes to objects, ideas, words, despair, justice, and memory.

These details fuel my journey through Washington to Seattle, where I spend the better part of the afternoon under a bridge waiting out the rain. The figurehead keeps me company with chatter, which is becoming more and more coherent with each passing mile. She talks the whole way along the California coast. "Immersed in natural waters," she says in one of her more lucid moments, "like the mollusk in marine phosphorescence. In me sounded the crusty salt forming my singular skeleton…I felt myself beating with it, my voice growing with the water."[2] After a long-haul trucker drops us warm and rested in Sacramento, we jump a southbound train that stops for an hour in L.A. As I type us down the coast, past the parks and beaches of San Diego to Mexico, she fills the empty boxcar with stories about armadas, sunken treasures, tides, and currents.

The guy manning the gate at the Tijuana border eyes the figure-head suspiciously and asks me what the purpose of my visit is. I offer the truth with as straight a face as I can manage. "That's impossible," he replies. "How can you visit Neruda? He's been dead for five years."

I smile at the confirmation that I have traversed thirty-nine years of time. I highlight the word "impossible" and hit delete.

That night, I close my eyes and dream that we ride a whale all the way down the Gulf of California, past the beachside promenade of Puerto Vallarta, through the coral reefs and shipwrecks of Manzanillo, and then on to the Guatemalan border.

The details regarding my sojourn through Central America involve a montage of border crossings, some by sunset, others by the light of the moon. I imagine great dangers, political unrest, and hurricanes, but instead we encounter beautiful and generous people. We are offered shelter in a Salvadorian village, where I am welcomed as a strange spectacle. My hosts laugh hysterically every time I am caught conversing with my peculiar cargo. Two days later, while negotiating with a Nicaraguan farmer for food, I have no choice but to insist the figurehead translates—her Spanish is much better than mine. We camp at the edge of a banana plantation in Costa Rica. There is a noticeable stoop in my posture now. Trekking along the Columbian coast with an icepack on my back, I write about the land and my impressions, but in the morning, she tells me that I have it all wrong. At a bus depot in Ecuador, as I'm wrapping duct tape around the hole that has formed in the sole of my left shoe, I notice a calendar which reads September 1976. A quick Internet search informs me that I have just missed a civilian uprising and the eruption of one of thirty active volcanoes. I need a rest, but wait until I'm in Peru before I press shift and hit the asterisk key.

■

Chile is a beautiful and diverse country, from the arid desert of the north to the stormy, rain-drenched forests of the south. It has a

2,610-mile coastline and therefore a strong affinity with the sea. We arrive in concert with a military uprising, during which the socialist leader is assassinated. From Santiago, we catch a bus to El Quisco and, as we walk the remaining miles along the shore, the figurehead is conspicuously silent; her voice, it seems, has been replaced by the waves breaking gently on the beach.

In the photo I had once seen, the fence around Neruda's house was a shrine—eulogies and greetings written in paint and pencil or carved into the wood with nails—but when we arrive, I am relieved to find that it is still a simple and unadorned, weatherworn, cedar boundary marking the edge of his property. I struggle up the path to his door, taking comfort that this time I know both how I got here and why I am here.

Once again I pause, barely able to bear the weight of the figurehead, and rest my weight on the railing. The door opens before I even knock and this time Neruda is wearing a fine, pinstriped suit, his bald head covered with a golfer's cap, and his feet clad in a pair of two-tone loafers. His eyes fall on the figurehead with a look of unabashed excitement. A long moment passes, during which I imagine some kind of secret communion transpiring between them. I wait patiently until he steps back and invites us in.

He leads us through a room with a green tiled floor, varnished tree trunks support the wood ceiling. I am so exhausted that I'm barely able to appreciate the wonder of what is happening. In the kitchen, he offers me a seat at a round, wooden table. The light from the window casts the room in a warm sepia glow as he casually uncorks and pours two glasses of red wine. I sigh heavily and perch awkwardly on the front section of the chair in order to allow room for the figurehead still secured to my back. He joins me at the table and we silently drink and eat tomatoes, biting into them like apples. When we are full of food and wine, he leads me to his study. Here, his demeanour shifts again and, like a child no longer able to contain himself, he offers to help me with the knotted rope securing the figurehead in place. As I rub the sore marks on my shoulders, Pablo carries her over to the window, speaking to her softly in Spanish. Several minutes pass before I realize that he is not conversing with her, but rather reciting a poem. He runs a hand gently along her cheek, leans in, and kisses her forehead, and then turns his attention back to me. "How can I repay you for such a gift?" he asks.

For a man who will be dead in a number of days, he looks good. I glance over at the figurehead. For a woman carved out of oak a few hundred years ago, she looks good too. They look good together and, while I am buoyed by this outcome, I am burdened by the fact that I can barely stand up. "I'm tired," I tell him, as I straighten my back. "I ask only one thing… finish the story for me."

"That's it? No money? No… autograph?" he adds, smiling.

"You have done enough," I tell him.

Pablo selects a book from the shelf and flips to a marked page as if he has done this a thousand times. "Ah yes, this will do," he says…

Today we picked you up from the sand
In the end, you were destined for my eyes.
Doubtless you're sleeping, sleeper, perhaps you're dead, deceased;
And the errant splendor has ceased its wandering.[3]

With four lines of poetry, I am back at my apartment, staring at the screen of my computer. The figurehead is home and I am home, the story—bits and pieces washed up on the page, some discarded, some of it the wrecks of other tales—flotsam and jetsam. As I type these last lines, I find myself wondering whose story this is. Am I writing it or am I being written? In the end, I take comfort in two things: in fiction anything is possible and my back no longer aches.

END NOTES:
1. Pablo Neruda, "The Dream" from *Los Versos del Capitan*
2. Pablo Neruda, "The Tides" from *El Fuego Cruel*
3. Pablo Neruda, "To a Ship's Figurehead" from *El Oceano*

SILENCE

I use Max's silver-plated Zippo to ignite a tightly scrunched section of the *International Herald Tribune*. We have already burned through an Ellery Queen novel and a map of Paris. The smoky flame of newsprint flickers, illuminating the damp, stone wall that surrounds us.

I manage to get some work done in that sputtering light—calmly, rationally, taking notes and drawing sketches with the pen and pad that were luckily in my shirt pocket, while Max, seemingly oblivious to the wonder and severity of our predicament, nonchalantly sips his wine, which was luckily in his backpack. You'd have thought he was sitting in a bistro in Montmartre the way he dabs his lips with a stained hanky before extracting a mangled wing from his mouth. They are everywhere—hundreds, possibly thousands of them resting on our shoulders, crushed under our shoes—an entomological phenomenon, a discovery that would surely earn me the Foundation's Thomas Say Award for systemics, morphology, and evolution. But first, I have to deal with four facts: one, this species of butterfly was supposed to be extinct; two, every time we move we are in danger of crushing several specimens; three, Max is getting drunk; and four, we are trapped at the bottom of a well.

"These little critters would make a fine salad topping if you ever run out of croutons," Max says, holding a wounded specimen close to the flame of the tightly twisted paper.

I know he is trying to provoke me; he rarely misses an opportunity.

"So much for extinction," he continues. "I suppose this discovery is going to make you famous in terms of—what do you call it—lepidorera study, not to mention the ecological hullabaloo."

Max and I have been brothers, well, all our lives, and after forty years, I was used to his inability to grasp the gravity of a situation.

"It could have something to do with why whales beach themselves," I speculate out loud. "Something to do with a malfunction or interference with their echolocation. Or maybe Verlaine was on to something and, in response to some survival instinct, they became nocturnal and have been hiding out in dark places like this well for the last fifty odd years—travelling by night—navigating by planetary alignments."

"Or this is some kind of a hallucination," Max counters. "Something in the Parisian water—a wonderland rabbit hole where you evoke your greatest fantasies."

I sigh. It is times like these when it is difficult to believe that he is my older brother, but I'm still not beyond the childish inclination to return his verbal spars.

"If that were true," I say, "then for you, this would be an Andy Warhol installation and we'd be sitting at the bottom of a giant can of Campbell's soup."

"Just be glad I had the good sense to come down after you with my backpack," Max says. He refills his glass and bites into the end of a baguette. "We'd be starving to death by now."

With our legs crossed, we have about a foot between us—enough room to picnic, but not enough to sleep or, as Max points out, certainly not enough room to do his daily yoga exercises. Looking straight up from the cold earth floor inspires a number of metaphors—a beckoning, yet inaccessible light at the end of the proverbial tunnel, or, as Max more optimistically notes, a romantic full moon, a complement to his afternoon déjeuner. As the flame sputters into small, rising, orange ashes, Max emits a long, monotone "om," leaving us once again in the thick pitch of darkness.

■

I am an entomologist. I study insects, more specifically, I specialize in butterflies—*Papilionidae*, *Lycaenidae*, and my favourite, *Nymphalidae*. I am in France studying the migratory instinct of the *Vanessa cardui*—the Painted Lady—part of a working holiday—slash—determining-if-my-wife-is-having-an-affair thing. The frequency of her business trips had recently increased and she seemed to be chronically suffering from a headache whenever I amorously manoeuvred myself towards her side of the bed. And then one day, halfway to work, I realized that I had left my cellphone on the kitchen table and I made a U-turn.

She was still home when I got there. And she was back in bed.

Neither of us spoke for an uncomfortable length of time.

"I think I've come down with something," she said.

The silence split open like tightly stretched plastic.

"Food poisoning maybe. I decided to go back to bed and sleep it off."

"Hmmm."

I leaned up against the doorframe and didn't say a word. I wasn't sure how to deal with this growing distance between us. I hated the idea, but something was telling me she was lying, withdrawing into the shady back alleys of secrets. She had allegedly worked late the night before and had stopped at her favourite sushi joint. I ate her leftovers and I felt fine. I scanned the floor for stray socks, an errant tie, a tell-tale cufflink, or a book of matches with an anonymous phone number. But the room was clean with the exception of a faint, musty funk in the air.

"Aren't you late for work, hon?"

I nodded, restraining the sudden urge to break down into a mess of tears, and tried desperately to channel this vulnerability into manly indifference.

Glancing at the calendar as I left, I noticed a flight to Paris booked for the following Thursday for one of her quarterly conferences. I grabbed my cellphone, did some quick juggling of some deadlines, secured a cat-sitter, booked time off for field research, and called my brother.

Max came along as a consultant. He had lots of time on his hands ever since he made his fortune trading commodities. He's a big kid really, a consummate bachelor, a voracious reader of crime pulp, always carrying a iPod, rock and roll leaking out of the headphones. He smokes expensive cigars, wears a fedora, and has a closet full of ridiculous T-shirts like, *I'm not as think as you drunk I am.* His favourite had a black tie screen-printed on the front. He wouldn't know a Bordeaux from a Pilsner, but he enjoyed the extravagance his wealth afforded him with a genuine simplicity. He came with me because I needed support; I needed his knowledge of the private-eye genre, but he only agreed after I reminded him that Jim Morrison was buried in Paris.

We laid out our plan on the plane somewhere over the Atlantic. We would locate the target (my wife), secure lodgings (preferably with a continental breakfast included), and, while I went about my business (checking weather patterns, capturing and tracking specimens, measuring flight speed, et cetera), Max would visit the museums, cafés, and graveyards of his choice. In the evenings, we would rendezvous back at the hotel and establish surveillance on the target's activities.

"The trick," Max said, "is to get a handful of fake business cards so you look legit while impersonating taxi drivers, flower delivery people, room service personnel, and the like. People never question the authority of a business card."

At the Charles de Gaulle International Airport, we rented mopeds in order to blend into the traffic. "The helmets will add to the disguise," Max noted. I insisted that Max get rid of the striped shirt and the early stages of a pencil moustache, but he absolutely refused to part with the beret.

We had managed to book a room on the third floor of an inconspicuous pension across from the hotel my wife was staying at. Max was committed to the game and spent long hours in the "stake out," his amateur-astronomer, 14x Tyco telescope pivoting between my wife's window and the hotel lobby.

Truth is, surveillance is boring work. It was, for the most part, an exercise in patience. The first two nights, my wife retired early, her lights going out on the sixth floor at around 10:15 pm. I had to resist the urge to wave when she approached the window to draw the curtains. It was strange watching her like that. I felt both excitement and shame. Part of me knew I was trespassing on her privacy, but this discrepancy was justified by the possibility of her infidelity. I couldn't think of any other way that I could bridge the distance that had grown between us.

On the third day, at Max's insistence, we embarked on a recognizance mission. I was tired of losing my traveller's cheques to Max's superior skill when it came to cheating at cards and so I agreed. We infiltrated the hotel kitchen by impersonating health inspectors. Max even sampled the *crème brûlée* simmering on the stove. I failed to see how any of this would benefit our mission outside of an opportunity for Max to practise his French and pocket some fine Brie from the walk-in. When we left the kitchen, we got momentarily lost in the labyrinth of basement halls before finally emerging through an employee entrance into the hotel bar. Max couldn't resist interrogating the sommelier. I then spent ten anxious minutes explaining the risk of being discovered while drinking in the hotel where my wife was staying.

"*Je ne peux pas comprendre,*" he said.

It took all the strength I had not to strangle him.

■

I should have known better than to leave Max alone, but he was still sleeping the next morning when my wife broke her routine and jumped in a taxi. I abandoned my fruit cocktail and followed her on the moped—a long, slow, aimless drive through the city along Rue de Rivoli, across Pont-Neuf to the Boulevard Saint Germain, before finally stopping in front of the Louvre. The smile on her face was naively sweet as she leaned in the window to pay the driver, who had obviously taken an exceptionally indirect route. It is strange watching someone you know without them knowing. You notice subtle nuances, their unconscious mannerisms; they seem more relaxed, more natural, and more beautiful. She was no longer my wife, but a thirty-seven-year-old woman alone in Paris; attractive, mysterious, and for all anyone knew—single. I imagined meeting her for the first time, our shoulders close as we inspected the Mona Lisa. (Is the Mona Lisa in the Louvre?) I imagined saying something witty and profound, some little known fact about Leonardo. Our eyes meeting, her lips puckering as they do when she is working on a crossword. And then, several years flashed by like snapshots clicking in my head: A wedding we couldn't afford, our first condo, two miscarriages, her return to school to finish an abandoned degree, the business trips...

I was close enough to see the little lines at the corner of her eyes as she squinted in the direction of the museum. I was close enough to notice that she wasn't wearing her wedding ring.

When I met up with Max back in our room that evening, he was fidgeting with a small bottle of nail polish.

"What's that?" I asked.

"Exhibit A," he said.

He held the little bottle up like a happy housewife in a commercial promoting a new-and-improved cleaning product. "I snuck into her room after the two of you left. Her room is very elegant, much nicer than this place. The bathtub is marble, there's two single beds, and if it's any comfort, they're about three feet apart," he said. "How was your day?"

"What the fuck, Max!" I couldn't contain myself. "Did you go through her underwear drawer too? This is my wife, remember." Despite the circumstances, I felt that my wife's bedroom, even if it was in a hotel, was my bedroom as well. Max was unfazed.

"It's a clue," he said.

"That's unprofessional," I scolded. "And besides, what if she misses it? Tomorrow we'll hand it to the concierge. Tell them you found it in the elevator."

"It's called 'deception blue,'" he said, tossing the bottle on the bed.

∎

I couldn't sleep that night. Maybe I was sobering up from the jealousy because I was beginning to feel foolish. I unscrewed the lid of the nail polish, dabbed a bit on the pinky of both hands, and blew on them as I had seen my wife do. The hard edge of my anger softened, my shoulders dropped, I felt like a dandy, like Oscar Wilde, or Ziggy Stardust. Deception blue is metallic, a deep rare shade, hard to compare to anything in the natural world except maybe the colour of eyes, my wife's eyes. I remembered being struck by them when we first met and I wondered when, at what moment, I stopped seeing how incredible they are. I examined my fingers by the window. I'd never seen her wearing anything this extravagant. Not since we were dating. Back when her hair was auburn, black clothes offset with tartan accessories in honour of her Scottish heritage, her ears pierced seven times. But she lost that tinge of an accent, no longer drinks beer, rarely wears nail polish, and when she does it's usually something conservative and red, not too bright, something to complement her lipstick. Was this part of some secret disguise, a part of her personality that she couldn't share with me? From our fourth floor perspective, I couldn't really make out what was happening in her room, so I was left to the cruel and vivid insecurity of my imagination.

I glanced down at the dark, empty street: the geranium boxes in the windows, parked cars, the tilted chairs on café patios. The sky was overcast, no stars, no moon, and on the sixth floor, second from the left, there was still no sign of my wife.

I was dozing in the chair, despite the rhythmic saw of Max's snoring, when he awoke suddenly with an epiphany.

"It's a woman." Max was on his feet; even in the dark, I could see that his boxers were twisted and riding low, his hair comically astray.

"She's sleeping with a woman. That explains the nail polish."

Tears welled in my eyes, but I pretended that I was asleep, increasing the volume of my breathing. I couldn't have that conversation. It didn't matter if it was a woman or a man; the point was that I wasn't sure that I wanted to know the truth. If I didn't say anything, I wouldn't be part of this anymore. I wanted to go back to the oblivion of ignorance. Silence was a way of not participating. It excluded me from the situation, gave me immunity from what might be revealed. As long as there was silence, there was room to speculate, and, in the safety of non-participation, there was the possibility of a happy outcome.

Max climbed back into bed, tugged the covers up, and turned to face the wall.

"Did you ever think that it might be your fault?" he said.

■

I felt an overwhelming sense of embarrassment and sadness as I watched the morning sun melt the ice cubes in my juice, congeal the marmalade on my croissant. Max had his nose buried in a French newspaper. He was ignoring me and I knew I owed him an apology, but the best I could do was surrender.

"Okay, it's over," I said. "I give up." Whoever it was she was sleeping with—man or woman—could have her. I probably didn't deserve her anyway.

But then my mind was at it again. How many times had she referred to my work as "another woman," a remark that was usually followed by a nervous laugh? Maybe there were clues, attempts to hint at the early stages of her affair. Perhaps they were only flirting back then, exchanging marital grievances. Maybe she wanted to get caught so that once and for all we could deal with the things we couldn't seem to say. But I missed the cues. "Yes," I would counter,

"I'm in love with Queen Alexandra," a reference to my favourite butterfly. "But don't worry," I would add, "she's extinct." And that's how I was treating our marriage vows, like some slightly humorous memory—a precious thing of the past.

"Take the rest of the day off." I told Max. "I need time to think. Go visit your grave."

The wall of newspaper between us crumpled, "No, no," he said. "God knows you need me now more than ever."

When I decided to call her on my cell, I was standing in a field in Montrouge, just on the outskirts of the city, plotting the flight direction of a cluster of Red Admirals on a rose graph. Max was lying on his back, looking at the clouds through the wrong end of my binoculars, *Love Me Two Times* muted and tinny hissing out of the headphones. I was feeling calm, rehearsing my nonchalant greeting before actually dialling. One last ray of hope pivoting on the simple possibility of whether she would mention visiting the Louvre, share something personal, tell me what it was like to stand before the Mona Lisa. And if she could manage this intimacy, all would be forgiven. I would ask her to come home.

A man's voice answered the phone.

"Who's this?" I asked.

There was a stutter and then some rustling on the end of the line before my wife's voice, high and flustered. I could feel the distance between us, the distance between everyone close to me. And in that pregnant moment of hopelessness, I couldn't decide if I was sad or angry. And once again, I couldn't bring myself to say anything meaningful. I just held the phone to my ear and listened to the drawn-out pause, the live connection of silence between us.

And then it happened.

A flicker of iridescent wing, a sparkle of blue like the swatch of my painted little fingernails came to rest on the lip of a milk thistle not more than two yards away. I had to remind myself to breathe. My heart pounded, my hands grew sweaty. I turned off the phone and slowly withdrew my guide to be sure. A wingspan of fifty-two to sixty millimetres, feeds on grape vines and soft fruits, migrates from Morocco in the spring, progeny returns south in autumn—but there have been no recorded sightings since 1972. *Papilio deceptis*, otherwise known as the Translucent Swallowtail is arguably the most beautiful and unique of its whole genus. The last reported sighting was by a young amateur collector by the name of Casper Verlaine who compared it to the cross-section of a sapphire. Registered on the Red List since the mid-1960s, Verlaine claimed to have chanced upon a cluster in a mine near Bordeaux. Having worked underground for the better part of his youth, he had extracted precious stones from deep and dark places, but never had he seen such a natural and exquisite wonder. Glimpsed on the wing, indeed it resembled the fractures of light caught in a rare stone, and when at rest, the simplicity of its design made it a unique and breathtaking specimen. Verlaine was seventeen, barely literate, and, despite the fact that his diary descriptions and sketches were extremely detailed and accurate, his sightings are largely held in the field with as much credibility as those of the Loch Ness monster.

It took all the concentration I could muster to keep from collapsing into the grass. I couldn't begin to express the personal and intimate depth of this occurrence. I started scribbling, recording cloud cover, temperature, details of wing, thorax and abdomen, latitude and longitude—my hand shaking as I wrote. When the specimen alighted from its perch, I took flight and followed it over a stone wall, through a stand of alders, and into the courtyard of an abandoned farmhouse where it came to rest momentarily on the edge of a well. I approached slowly, net at the ready. I paused. It paused. I tested the wind, raised the net, but it evaded my first approach, fluttered erratically in the light broken into rays by the surrounding trees, changed direction in haphazard zigzags, adjusted to imperceptible air currents, and then, nightmare of nightmares, it disappeared down into the shadowy darkness.

■

I had no idea how long I was unconscious, but I suppose I was lucky the well was dry. It was pitch black. I closed my eyes and focussed on each part of my body to determine what hurt the most. Three fingers were badly shredded on both hands; they had done little to impede my descent once my Birkenstocks lost their footing. My new prescription frames held up to the fall very well and, despite a mild headache, so had I. That is until Max came down after me.

"I jumped," he said matter-of-factly. His voice sort of echoed in the dark.

"What, no hesitation, no investigation, no assessment whatsoever?"

He shrugged his shoulders. "I saw your backpack up there. I called down to you but there was no answer," he said. "Jesus Christ, I thought you were dead for sure."

I was torn between Max's selfless concern for my wellbeing and the obvious repercussions of his choice to follow me into the well instead of going for help.

"Holy shit, Max!" I shouted. "I just can't trust you to do anything right."

It wasn't until Max had lit one of his foul-smelling cigars that we noticed the butterflies. The walls were literally breathing with *Papilio deceptis*, the ground a writhing mess of wounded and dead.

"You don't trust anybody," Max sighed.

■

Max opens a second bottle of red and, as I perform an autopsy on a dead but undamaged specimen, he nudges me with his foot.

"Maybe she's having an affair with an etymologist and the whole thing is a simple typographical misunderstanding—etymologist, entomologist—get it?"

I start thinking about my wife for the first time since the phone call. I imagine the conversation when I get home, me leaning up against the doorframe of our bedroom, dangling the blue bottle of nail polish between my fingers. Her tell-tale skin, a subtle red flush of guilt.

Silence.

"Okay, now what?"

Silence.

"Say something," she would demand. "It's like you don't give a shit."

Her guilt would need the climax that my silence denied her. I would refuse to break, to allow her the power of betrayal. I imagine my wife with her knees pulled up, the sheets held in clenched fists under her chin. "We don't talk anymore."

"That's it," Max says. "Nothing left to burn." Our eyes meet and I can see in that last moment of light that even he, who was so oblivious, seems a little worried.

We watch the little yellow ashes rise up towards the circle of light.

"Now what?" he asks, a voice in the darkness.

I had made a clumsy discovery, the result of a series of misguided actions. What I would do with this information would drastically affect my career, but for some reason, at the bottom of a well, this thought leaves me feeling empty. And then it dawns on me that this may be the end. What if we are never found?

"When we were kids," I say, "I don't know, nine or ten years old, we had bunkbeds at the time. Do you remember that?" Max doesn't answer. "You got to sleep on the top and I hated that because I always figured the creepy things that lurked under the bed would get me first." Truth is, I'm still afraid of the dark but I don't mention that. "Anyway," I continue, "it was pitch black like this, and I remember waking up from a nightmare and I was sort of sobbing in the dark, and you whispered my name. I just lay there in bed, pretending I was asleep because I was terrified that if I made a sound, whatever it was that was hiding in the darkness would know where I was."

I hear the thug of air as Max finishes gulping straight from the bottle, the glass abandoned in the inky blackness.

"I remember," he says. "I was afraid of the dark too, but I just wanted to let you know that I was there."

I want to reach out and touch his shoulder, to thank him. But instead I withdraw into the darkness, into the quiet of contemplation, into the thick comfort of it, the years vapourizing into meaninglessness, the darkness folding into itself until we are kids again, alone listening to the mysterious sounds of unseen things, frightened and fascinated, waiting to be saved by the morning light.

I imagine the butterflies carrying us out, their tiny tarsal hooked into the knit of our clothes, thousands of wings in unison lifting our bodies slowly into the air. We rise up in a swirling thermal, engulfed in a cloud of extinct *Papilionidae*. I imagine that we are weightless, ascending towards the heavens, high above the well, gazing out at the countryside, the vineyards to the south, Paris to the north, home to the west. And I smile when I see a little boy prop his bike up on the kickstand, nudge the backpack leaning against the well with his shoe, and then call down into the darkness.

"I love you." The words come out pointy, jumbled, each letter scratching the back of my throat. I can't see him in the darkness, but I know he is awake. I can hear him breathing. Max doesn't say anything, and I am glad. It was good to speak those words to him, let them linger in the air. I can hear Max shift his weight, I can feel the comfort of his presence and I wonder if I had ever been so kind to him before. But more than this, without diminishing the meaning in my declaration, I know, and I think that he knows too, that I am really only practising for when I get home.

A FEW WORDS OF LATIN

There was a time when I would enter the courtroom as if it were the helm of a magnificent ocean-going vessel—polished brass and mahogany, bow to stern. I would seize the rudder and steer the procession into the waves, turning to the jury as if they were a disciplined but anxious crew, and I, their captain.

The practice of law is a game of manipulation, rhetoric, and good seamanship. Indictment is a port of call, a place to anchor, however briefly, in a storm. But it has come to my attention that I've been taking in water, have been for some time now. What started with a slight list on the starboard side has grown into a debilitating drift, which has left me floundering in a squall of gin martinis. Lately, even the formalities of good cocktail mixology have been compromised. For example, the superbly dry martini I have just consumed was created without ice or a single olive.

And now I am lying on my back on my office floor. The water in the 1,200-litre saltwater tank I had installed to commemorate my first big win in the courts is sloshing against and occasionally breaching the glass. And while the two varieties of angelfish, a score of basslets, three dozen gobies, tangs, a large school of anthias, and a few dragonets swim about in a state of obliviousness, I hold fast against what I am certain is the approach of a class 9 storm. The question of whether it's best to abandon ship or just surrender and go under has been troubling me for days. But as I am still uncertain to which manner my nature is inclined, I turn my attention to the receiver of the phone that I left dangling over the edge of my desk when the pitch of the sea threw me to the floor. My wife's voice is tinny, anxious, and agitated.

"—You've really gone off the deep end, Jack. I think you need to see someone."

The silence that follows this plea gives way to what I recognize as the Mephisto Waltz No. 1, a classical piece that Nancy plays on our Steinway when she's upset. I can picture her sitting in front of the piano with her cellphone resting between her shoulder and her chin. Her manicured fingers moving, in my estimation, a tad bit earnestly across the keys.

"... and what's with all this drowning stuff?"

She's multitasking now. Playing and giving me hell at the same time.

"—You're a Libran, for God's sake. You're not even a water sign—"

The distance between us has become palpable—like sea air—and, as I lie there on the carpet in a briny fog, I drift into a memory that places me in my last year of high school, when I was still flirting with the idea of law—the formality, the finality—testing its ballast. I was presenting a paper on criminal justice entitled "Ethics and Jurisprudence," which argued in favour of a social anarchy borrowed and bastardized from the vodka-swilling intellectuals of the turn of the century. I closed my essay with the caveat, *summum ius summa inuria*—the more law, the less justice—a few words of Latin that I thought might give my satiric paper a pseudo-academic credibility. As I returned to my seat, I heard a voice whisper, "Latin is a sexy and elegant language." Nancy, who sat in the desk to my left, had never even spared me a glance until then and I found her sudden attention, no matter how quietly expressed, intoxicating.

After class, she accosted me in the hall, pinned me up against a locker, and then, leaning into the water fountain next to us she took a quick drink. The next thing I knew, she had her hand on my crotch and she was kissing me. I remember trying to breathe as her tongue eagerly explored the architecture of my mouth. The whole thing was over in a matter of seconds, but the effects of that collision left me delirious. Who knew that a few words of a dead language could elicit such a lusty response?

Nancy convinced me to become a lawyer on our first date. She argued that reason and justice were two edges of the same sword and who better than a Libran to wield such a thing? "The courts," she declared, "are a place where a man can make a difference and a decent living." We married the week after I passed the bar. She had insisted on waiting. "I had to be sure," she said, never elaborating on whether she was referring to her feelings or the question of whether I could actually pass the exam.

When the money started coming in, she stopped reading horoscopes and took up tennis. She gave up lemon gin for wines from the Grand Cru Vineyards in France. And she spent hours on the Internet perusing the sites of celebrity-endorsed interior designers. She came home one day with a fake tan and insisted on a trip to New York, something about a piano dealer named Faust Harrison. Our second-hand Yamaha had suddenly become an embarrassment. During the next eight years, we acquired a mortgage on a too-large house in a gated community, we holidayed at Kuoni Collection-recommended luxury resorts and dined at Forbes-rated restaurants. I can still see Nancy exchanging stories with her friends over spritzers at the club, tilting her tennis racket back over her shoulder, and then, with a flick of her wrist, illustrating how she cast the imaginary line.

I had been caught, gutted, stuffed, and mounted.

Nancy's voice on the phone is getting louder, moving, I am sure, towards some kind of ultimatum.

"—I don't care about the car, Jack. I just want my life back."

She's referring to the Jaguar, which I traded in yesterday for a Nissan that started with a cough and left a black stain on the asphalt of the used car lot—like trading a yacht for a rowboat, I know, but the F-Type was murder on maintenance and I was behind on payments. After freeing up some capital on the trade, I stopped at the bank to assure Nathan, who manages my portfolios, that there was no reason to panic and then I headed over to Mickey's where I had a couple quick cocktails to—calm the panic. The next thing I knew I was parked on the esplanade, watching the waves break on the lakeshore. I couldn't take my eyes off the horizon. Though I couldn't see it, I knew the tsunami was coming.

Nancy was waiting for me when I finally got home. Even she could tell the difference between the sweet purr of a $70,000 coupé and the economical choke of a midsize compact.

"Whose car is that?" she asked when I stepped in the door.

I glanced at the pile of messages accumulating on my cellphone, loosened my tie, and told her that I was getting too old for the flash. She was blissfully oblivious to the state of our finances and yet she had an acute awareness when it came to the quality and status of everything we possessed.

"A fucking *Sentra*, Jack?"

I looked at my watch—I still have the Rolex—as if I was late for something and then left her in the hallway steadying herself on the oak wood banister of the staircase.

"What's next, Jack, a moped?"

It wasn't until I passed through the living room that I noticed that she had moved the furniture again. The kitchen table was where the couch used to be and she had managed to get my dresser down the stairs and into the dining room. God only knows what she had done with the television.

I made my way up to the bathroom where I locked the door and popped a few Valium and high doses of B complex vitamins, which turned my urine the colour of a Lemon Neon Tetra. My reflection in the mirror undulated back at me as if I were under water. As I listened to what sounded like my wife dragging the mattress and box spring out into the hall, I stripped off my clothes and stepped into the empty tub.

It was still dark when I woke up. My legs were cramped and my back was aching as I climbed into the same clothes I had worn the day before. I made my way downstairs and took a look out the living room window. Outside, a ceiling of ominous clouds obscured the stars. Wet leaves were swirling across the yard. I pulled up my collar and, as I headed to the kitchen, I could feel the floor rocking gently to and fro. In order to get to the cupboard, I had to squeeze past the love-seat that was jammed up against the stove. The Steinway was now in front of the dishwasher and the fridge had been moved into the centre of the room where the table and chairs used to be. I knew that all this furniture moving was, though neurotic and brutal, Nancy's way of coping. By rearranging all this stuff—luxury designer, brand name furniture and appliances—she was trying to get my attention, force me to engage. But it had been years since we had sat down with a bottle of wine to verbally hash out the little tensions that, left unspoken, accumulatively complicate a marriage. And now, it was simply too late. Indulgence and neglect had incrementally taken their toll. The end was imminent.

As I sat at the piano bench, slowly munching on granola, middle C and B flat droning quietly like a distant foghorn under the weight of the bowl, I took inventory of the day ahead: appointments, retainers, opening statements, disclosures, summations, demonstrating evidence, closing statements...mayday.

When I heard my wife's footsteps coming down the stairs, I reached for my coat, but the narrow space between the Steinway and the damn Rosso Verona counter slowed me down enough that she caught me at the door.

"Jack, we have to talk."

A sharp pain twisted deeply in my solar plexus as Nancy moved towards me. I reached into my jacket pocket and pulled out the flask I started carrying a few weeks ago. I took a quick swig and chased it with two mints.

Nancy shook her head slowly. "Jesus Christ, Jack, what is going on?"

A few drops of rain hit the window.

"*I sentio amo I concaluit,*" I said.

Nancy stared at me, her lips tight, waiting for me to elaborate, but that was the long and short of it.

"*You feel like you're drowning*—so you do *feel* something, then?"

She followed this rhetorical question with a barrage of complaints that focussed primarily on either my absence or what she called a "withdrawal into silence." As her voice grew more exasperated with each itemized point, the room began to tilt. I reached for the counter and as she went on, I could see her words rippling like a giant wave towards me. I pushed the door open and stepped out into the rain.

How I made it to work safely, I can't be sure. I have no memory of the drive, but when I entered the building, I discovered that my clothes were soaking wet and that my lungs ached with each breath. Heads turned as I made my way to my office.

When I opened the curtains, the city seemed out of focus. I stared at the rising water eight stories below, the grey clouds above. I was due in court in three hours, but as I turned my mind to the work at hand, the room began to tilt again. A lamp toppled, water from the fish tank sloshed onto the carpet. When I looked back out the window, I saw that the storm had arrived. A howling wind preceded what I could feel was the approach of the seismic wave I had been anticipating.

My secretary stuck her head in the door as I was trying to keep my balance whilst pouring a decent shot of gin.

"Sorry," she said. "But...your wife is on line one."

I was at that moment distracted by the sad realization that there was no ice and I was out of olives.

"Everything okay?"

"Fine, fine," I said, adding a splash of vermouth.

"Smells sort of briny in here."

I glanced back at the window just as the wave appeared on the horizon. I downed the martini. "Yes," I said, reaching for the phone. "Better batten down the hatches."

■

"It's over, Jack. I want a divorce."

Nancy's voice, muted and static, is distant now, like a transmission breaking miles away. I pull myself up from the carpet and adjust my tie. I can feel what is left of my waterlogged heart stutter and then go dead.

"Jack? Are you there, Jack?"

The hum of the pump and filter draws my attention back to the tank. The coloured gravel, the anchored kelp, the coral, the strategically placed rocks and porcelain ornamentations, the splendid detachment of the fish.

I right a toppled chair, drag it across the carpet, step up, and, as I peer into the water, they come to the surface to greet me, unblinking eyes, emotionless—their only objective is to eat and not get eaten.

Descende cum nave.

I don't bother to remove my clothes because they are already soaking wet.

"Captain Jack Brill," I whisper, as I step into the tank, "*is going down with the ship.*"

ABERRATIONS

I hate winter. Especially here on the west coast where each slog of a day plays out against a backdrop of low light and drizzle. I bundle up each morning with a plaid scarf wrapped around my throat, a watchman's tuque pulled low over my ears, and make my weary way to work under the shelter of an umbrella. My pale skin and reptilian blood are not suited for the damp chill of life on the coast, which is to say nothing about the inflated rents and the thin stretch of a student loan, all of which I contend with for the simple reason that this city is the home of the only university in the country that would have me. I am a philosopher by nature, a barista by necessity, an observer of the quirks and routines of life at the front lines of where the urban morning begins. But I haven't always supplemented my academic career as a purveyor of caffeinated beverages. I've done brief entrepreneurial stints as a fortuneteller, a mime, and as a magician. I've got the business cards to prove it. But coffee is more reliable—flexible hours, tips, a steady paycheque, and an intimate and controlled environment in which to test my theories in the field—skim milk, mocha latte, hold the cinnamon, Americano tall, cappuccino, extra whipped cream. There is a certain amount of predictability in the rotation, but every once in a while something (Kierkegaard would say God, but my man Hume would argue for chance) throws a spanner in the works. Anomalies appear, the tempo shifts, and there's a new configuration in the cycle. These aberrations fascinate me. And that is the essence of what my thesis explores: how fate, will, and chance shape who and what we become.

■

Around the time that my mime prospects were waning, I found myself photocopying my resume once again. Rent was due and I had recently worn a hole in the soles of my rubber boots, so I applied for a job at one of those ubiquitous franchises where the coffee is bitter, the biscotti tastes like petrified cardboard, and you need a prerequisite BA just to get an interview. I was overqualified, but their washrooms needed cleaning so they hired me on the spot. If it weren't for this lucky break, I wouldn't have flunked out of university, I wouldn't be where I am today, freezing my ass off on this wet sidewalk, and I never would have met my fiancée.

Lin worked at the club a few doors down from my new place of employment. She called herself an "exotic entertainer." Heaven forbid you use the word stripper, she'd give you a lashing—a vicious verbal assault pointed with Cantonese expletives. "It's a business," she would say. "I take my clothes off and put them back on, and I get paid. The rest is all illusion and fantasy, somebody else's, not mine."

I occasionally patronized her place of employment. But in all honesty, I was there for the solitude—it was a place to hide out. You see, I was sleeping with my theology prof at the time (that was back during my Epicurean period) and we would have these fights, and well, I knew she would never look for me there. So every once in a while, after a shift at the coffee shop, I'd slide into a booth at Sully's, order a ten-dollar beer, open a volume of Hume, and tap away at the keys of my Underwood portable typewriter until they kicked me out.

I don't know what it was that made Lin focus her mannequin eyes on me. There were always a handful of eager boys drinking Heinekens at the front with their baseball caps, erections, and wallets at the ready, while I was working at my thesis as far away from the action as I could get. I admit that I had noticed her blue wig, which in itself separated her from all the other naked bodies that labouriously haunted the stage, and it did inspire me to ponder the juxtaposition of both disguising yourself and revealing yourself at the same time. But I was oblivious to the fact that she was Asian, curvy, and a little bit older than the other girls until she slid in across from me, her bare legs squeaking against the vinyl seat. "What are you reading?" she asked, tucking a Rothmans between her red, red lips.

I felt strange mixture of embarrassment and excitement, as if I had been found out, discovered.

When she saw that I made no move to close the book, she squinted her eyes at me, looked down at the page curling out of the typewriter, "Ah Philosophy for Idiots," she said.

I gave her points for being able to read upside down, but I was neck deep in a short but intense chapter on probability and chance and I felt vaguely uncomfortable talking to a stranger who, aside from a few inches of fabric, was naked. My eyes paused on the faded butterfly tattooed on her left breast and then settled for another brief moment on her lips. I felt bad. Up close I could see that she looked tired, almost thirty, the *Papilionidae* slightly distorted by the stretching of skin. "I'm just here for the cheap beverages," I said.

"I liked you better when you didn't speak," she said.

I don't know what she expected of me, but it was clear that I wasn't doing whatever it was I was supposed to be doing properly because she tossed the cigarette at me, which hit my forehead and landed between pages 136 and 137 of my second-hand volume of *An Enquiry Concerning Human Understanding*. As she walked away, I could see that the bench left a red mark on her legs between the backs of her knees and the impressive curve of her ass. She turned, as if she knew I would be looking, and gave me the finger.

■

A week later, on a wet Sunday afternoon, I found myself back at Sully's. She was sitting at the bar with a light blue cardigan pulled over her shoulders, smoking a cigarette. I don't know what compelled me, but I found myself asking the waitress to send her a shot of Jägermeister. When the drink arrived, she climbed off her stool, wove her way through the maze of empty tables, and placed the shot on the table next to my typewriter. "If you want to buy a girl a drink," she said, "don't waste your money on something that tastes like cough syrup." Before I could respond, she squeezed into the seat across from me and told me that her drink of choice was tequila.

Between our fourth and fifth shot, I realized that we had met before. It was during my first shift at the coffee shop, in the midst of a mid-day rush, the cappuccino machine whining and huffing over the din, when she walked in the door. She was wearing a faux fur hat, a crushed velvet periwinkle coat, black leggings, and combat boots. The mystery of the Orient in her coffee-black eyes as she made her way past the display of Bodums and eco mugs. The manager sent me, the new guy, to enlighten her about how the washrooms were for the use of paying customers only. I was eager to please, so I leaned myself casually against the sage-green wall next to the Modigliani print and waited for her outside the washroom door. When she saw me standing there in my mocha-coloured smock, logo embroidered across the bib, she stopped and crossed her arms. I was determined to communicate in a way that mimicked the absurdity of the situation, and so I started with my glass wall routine just to get warmed up—how I stumbled from the French existentialists to the silent art of Marcel Marceau is, despite what the existentialists would say, another example of pure chance, and a story too long to decant— but by the time I was feigning a rather strenuous bowel movement she raised her fist, ejected her index finger, and headed out the door. Not a word was spoken, but we understood each other perfectly. I was impressed.

The philosophy of mime is at its heart the practice of making concrete realities abstract, and now here we were again, several months later, with a scattering of shot glasses between us, communicating through another form of abstraction that confirmed that Lin was an unhappy woman; it was there both in the music she danced to and in her eyes. And while sadness is not in my opinion a very alluring trait, her capacity for juxtaposition and irony was impressive. When she took off her wig, she surprised me again. "In China," she said, "the butterfly is the emblem of love, long life, happiness, and beauty. It is the gift a man gives a woman when they marry."

"A dowry," I interjected.

She nodded. "But more than this, it represents transformation, the emergence of one's potential." It was then that she turned her attention to the stage. "I got this tattoo to remind me every time I take my clothes off that I am in a state of becoming."

I confessed then and there that I wasn't much into the Eastern philosophies. "Yin Yang, Zen, and all that stuff," I said, "are too ethereal—too many metaphors. I needed something I can nail down with the fist of my conviction." And that was when she leaned over, as if to identify some anomaly on my chin, and kissed me. And as if by some ancient Eastern hocus-pocus, I gave up one unhappy lover for another.

Three months later, we were living together. I showed up with two suitcases—1970s Samsonite—the orange one full of clothes, the lime-green one full of books. She wasn't home when I arrived, a disappointment that would be typical of our relationship. She worked nights and slept most of the day, while I was an early riser and spent my time fuelling the caffeine-addicted populace and working on the thesis. Most of our time together was spent in passing, our fragmented conversations ending prematurely, much like our sex life on the random occasions when we found ourselves in bed and awake at the same time.

But over time, routine leads to carelessness and the odds swing against you. While I had become quite adept at using a purely cerebral stance to protect my heart (Bertrand Russell would have been proud), the longer we were together, the more complacent I grew.

And for a while, I was blissfully oblivious and self-absorbed, going about my life much as I had when I was on my own. But nothing stays the same and, as if to prove this point, Lin started coming at me from weird angles, silent, peripheral appeals that completely defied my rational strategies. She started leaving little clues scattered around the apartment, torn-out pages from catalogues of matching towel sets tucked into my copy of *Thus Spoke Zarathustra* on the back of the toilet, a photo of a butterfly stuffed into my favourite coffee mug, a red circle around a three-stone ring taped to the milk carton in the fridge. But it wasn't until she reverted to a more aggressive form of communicating that I fully grasped what it was she trying to tell me.

The first thing she ever threw at me was the cigarette that night in Sully's; the second was the news that her period was late. I tried to duck, but she caught me in the chest, bullseye, just to the left.

I'm not sure what philosophical train of thought I was following at the time, but I got very drunk that night. I wandered aimlessly in the rain until I was miserable and soaked to the bone. And though I can't remember if I stumbled or intentionally bent to one knee, when I got home I proposed to her.

And I think I was happy for a moment in that cheap Hollywood dream, a drug that left me so discombobulated that I felt compelled to call my parents, look up old friends, go to a high school reunion, as if getting married and being a family man were things I had always aspired to. But as everyone knows, all highs lead to a hangover. And while Lin negotiated her hormones and I contemplated the meaning of fatherhood, we fell into a habit of brief and cutting dialogue and, with all subtlety and pretense abandoned, it was obvious that neither of us was equipped to be a parent.

"I need your half of the rent," she said, after shaking me awake.

My mind shifted to the down payment I had secretly laid out on the ring. "Can you wait till Friday?" I offered.

She shook her head. "When are you going to finish that fucking thesis?"

I turned to the window and looked out at the rain-smeared world. The plan had always been to get as far away from here as I could as soon as I finished my doctorate—get a job in a desert maybe, somewhere warm and dry—but things had come to a halt. I was neck deep in writer's block and the baby meant I wasn't going anywhere. "Lin Wong," I said. I used her full name when I wanted to make a point. "We need to talk."

She retreated to the doorway.

I got out of bed and followed her down the hall as far as the kitchen. I needed a coffee, a moment to gather my thoughts, but Lin had launched into a cupboard-slamming fit that made me want to make her disappear, turn her into a rabbit, or otherwise exercise what she would call my "Yang element." But instead, I found myself, apropos of nothing, quoting the Paris-born Henri Bergson's book *Creative Evolution*, in which he wrote, "To exist is to change, to change is to mature, to mature is to go on creating oneself endlessly."

The third thing Lin threw at me was the news that she had had an abortion. Her voice was just loud enough to be heard above the sound of my breaking heart, which was followed by a high-pitched shriek as she ripped in two my annotated copy of *A Treatise on Human Nature*. I'm not sure what the fourth thing she threw at me was, but it hit me in the back of the head as I was stepping out the door.

As I stumbled through the rain, I couldn't shake the thought that I had been adopting other people's philosophies for so long that I had lost touch with myself. I had been living outside, pursuing a degree as if it were the key to a secret door that would open to reveal whatever greatness I contained within. But all I could feel was the weather, the damp chill of existential loneliness, and the impending doom of my academic deadlines.

I purchased a two-pound bag of espresso, a carton of cigarettes, a ream of recycled typewriter paper, and two weeks later I had twenty-seven pages of footnotes, quotes, and cross-references, a bibliography that covered two millennia, and a sore back from sleeping on the beer-stained couch of an equally down-and-out friend.

The night before I was scheduled to defend, I found myself drifting past Sully's. I took one of those seats in the back and watched Lin perform for the first time. And true to her claim that the audience had nothing to do with it, I saw the subtle adjustments between the hurt and the power. I saw that everything she did was a reaction to something that had happened before. Her slow and deliberate removal of clothing was as purposeful as preparing for a shower—there was nothing erotic about it. Her amulet had lost its power. And I was reminded of Locke's *Tabula Rasa*. The clean slate, the canvas from which to begin. Begin. A new journey, a new life. How long do butterflies live, I wondered. From where I sat, the tattoo was a smudge on her breast.

I slipped out the door. A light drizzle blown by a heavy wind snuck up the cuffs of my coat and chilled my skin. With every step, I could feel the resistance and gravity of the season, a downpour that forced my eyes to the ground. And that's when it occurred to me that making a fine mochaccino could be the most valuable thing I had ever done. The fuel that feeds the machine that is our society. Without it, universities would collapse, office work would slow to a standstill, thousands of educated people would be out of work.

∎

I woke with a dreadful hangover, red paint on the tips of my fingers, and, as I dragged myself into the kitchen, I realized that I was late for my defence. I skipped breakfast, threw on my coat, scarf, and hat, and hurried out the door. The morning was calm. The low clouds obscuring the tops of the buildings, cars sliding by with a muted hiss. My coat was still damp from the night before, but the promise of a hot coffee fuelled my detour all the way to the coffee shop where I worked. There was a closed sign on the door, yellow police tape across the entrance. Through the broken glass, I could see that somebody had vandalized the cappuccino machine, spray-painted aphorisms all over the walls. I glanced down at the paint on my hands and ran.

I arrived at the university out of breath, hurried down the hall, and pushed open the door with a forced grin. I peeled off my damp jacket and, as I caught a glimpse of myself in the window's reflection, I realized what a mess I was. I apologized for my tardiness, acutely aware of my insincerity, I was repulsed by the temperature and texture of each hand that I shook. "Good morning" echoing in my ears until the meaning dropped out. It was like when you say the simplest word over and over, eventually it seems as if you have never heard that word before; you can't even spell it. The certainty of its meaning evaporates. I looked at my advisor, the External, the Chair, the audience, and I couldn't remember what I had planned on saying. I had lost my bearings. And along with this cerebral amnesia came an uncertainty of time and place—the second, the minute, and the year suddenly exclaiming their arbitrary value. Something was shifting, the stars were out of whack, the cycle was broken, and, in the back of my mind, a million butterflies were flapping their wings.

Sometimes change is a graceful thing, sometimes it'll leave you stupefied in a profound and irrational epiphany in front of an expecting audience, and sometimes it will take an old wrench and twist the brass eagle off the top of the cappuccino machine, inspire your hand to the unsolicited expression of the subconscious—a vandalized manifestation of the inner self. What the caterpillar calls the end, the butterfly calls the beginning.

I could see the Chair reach for his tie, give the knot a tug as he rotated his head slightly from side to side. My advisor, representatives from the department, and fellow students sat in an uncomfortable silence as I pushed my chair back and climbed up onto the table. The room was caught in a moment of digestion. But everything I had been studying suddenly revealed something new to me. That all this was a form of simulated masturbation. Academic indulgence. Elitist and steeped in theory. In this room, the real world seemed far away, quartered off by centuries of self-indulgent theoretical study. An audience and a stage. What value do ideas have if the people expressing them are simply performing? All I could think about was Lin taking off her clothes for an audience of drunken strangers. And that was it. My defence was fractured by a postmodernist insight. I started with my shirt, button by button, and I slowly, deliberately removed my clothes to reveal my wings.

Nature was playing tricks on herself. It felt like spring, but it wasn't. The warm sun stimulated the dormant spirit within—crocuses, daffodils and cherry blossoms. It was the kind of day that you have to watch your step, keep an eye out for open manhole covers and falling pianos. I removed my scarf, unbuttoned my coat. I could smell the earth from the square footings of the trees that lined the sidewalk, steam was rising from the tops of cars wet with dew. I had managed to bum enough for a coffee and, as I was peeling back the lid on my extra-large, organic, shade-grown Columbian, I spotted a butterfly. It was resting on a parking meter, ruminating on the intoxicating exhaust fumes emitting from the muffler of an idling Volvo. Its neon-blue abdomen arced, jade wings slowly vacillating, and I was amazed, I mean, when was the last time you saw a butterfly in the city, let alone in January? As I sipped my coffee, I confess I was captivated by the creature's ageless beauty. I exhaled and the white mist of my breath engulfed the insect and left it glistening in the low morning light. It raised its wings as if it were about to fly away and, without the slightest signal, it expired—frozen, dead, kaput. There was no complaint, no withering or resistance, just a strange kind of instinctual surrender. I considered the philosophical and superstitious values of the event and I decided that it was a gift, not a curse.

I crouched and leaned back against the meter, placed the Underwood down on the sidewalk, took off my gloves, and began typing. The words on the napkin tucked into the carriage bled a little, but were as legible as my thoughts. The crudeness of the situation inspired me, knowing I could blow my nose with this story or, if things got bad enough, use it to wipe my ass. I took another sip of coffee and I glanced up at the trickery of the sun and its promise of warmth and spring. I had hit rock bottom and yet, somehow I felt as if I was weightless, floating above the cool cement. My fingers tapping away at the Underwood—I hate winter. I pulled my toque down low and I was glad to see clouds gathering on the horizon, comforted in the certainty that the cold rain would wash away any confusion as to whether or not this was simply another beautiful winter day.

STILL LIFE WITH ROTTEN FRUIT

The last thing you remember is placing your hands in the water. It was opening night at the Savoy Theatre—a near sellout—a one-act monologue about a Houdini-like escape from the metaphorical confines of housewifery, the tentacles of the appliance's power cords binding you to the slave trade of 1950s patriarchal values. As you went about your daily chores, illuminated by a hot spotlight, you dragged the entangled appliances behind you—an iron, toaster, blender, microwave oven—symbolic extensions of your limbs. At the end of the first act, you stumble over to the sink and the waiting pile of dishes, only to find that one of the theatre's custodians had made toast earlier that day running an extension cord from the men's washroom to the prop. There was no scream, just a flash, the lightning arc of your spine jolting backwards, the thump of your body hitting the stage, and a fine wisp of blue smoke rising from your lips into the darkness.

■

Andy

The whole thing was very upsetting. Some people in the audience actually thought it was part of the show and began to applaud. I was the first one at Liza's side and, though I was relieved when she opened her eyes, she looked at me as if we were strangers, a look of astonishment and horror, a look that I would recognize in the coming months more frequently than I would care to admit. She was so talented, chameleon-like, so full of energy, but I had never seen her put on a performance like that before. I like to think we balanced each other, my practicality and voice of reason to her creative and sometimes hysterical moodiness. She once told me that my greatest asset was my ability to not compromise her vision. "I've dated other artists," she told me, "but they're too high maintenance. You, on the other hand, are so blissfully uncomplicated." And it was true. While she was brooding about a production's dramaturge or a particularly troubling script, manically binging on potato chips or otherwise engaged in her creative processes, I'd flip through one of the vegetarian cookbooks she kept in a red milk crate under her kitchen sink and make sure she had a decent meal—a good balance of proteins and carbs and all that. I never took Liza to task, never bothered her about her hoarding tendencies and, when things heated up as they sometimes did, I'd simply disappear back to my apartment and check the climate a few days later. I confess I never really understood her art, but I knew it meant a lot to her and I knew better than to wear my baseball cap to her openings. I'd say we were pretty happy. Before the accident. Before Agatha.

■

Agatha

And that is why this story does not belong to him. He is obliviously unable to appreciate both Liza's unique talent and the gift that she was to the world—the kind of guy who keeps his socks on when he makes love. He could never relate to Elizabeth the way I could. It took a photographer's eye. Andy couldn't understand that my appreciation for her was beyond physical. She was my muse. Liza the artist had become art itself. Capturing the essence of Liza required an expert harmony of aperture, shutter, and film speed, that and a heavy dose of goddamn luck.

■

Your skin has had a translucent quality to it ever since the spectacular tragedy. You are, according to the doctors, a miracle—a veritable circulatory X-ray of milky veins running the length of your body, the fibrous ridges of your brachioradialis, a schematic of arteries, tendons, and nerves

defining your arms and legs. "Stay out of the sun," they said after count-
less biopsies—you see grapes turning to raisins.

What they don't know is that you experience everything as a
memory now. You are never present—even this realization is a memory.
Everything seems to unfold slower than it should—you are always too late.

In the vague blizzard of the coma, you remember a garden, an
orchard of fruit—is it biblical—a sense of liberation—Buddhist maybe?
You want to go back to that place and stay forever. Every time you close
your eyes, you are surprised by what you see when you open them. You
catch a frightening glimpse of yourself in the mirror and think, if man
is made of clay, what is woman made of—something different for sure.
You eye an apple core on the windowsill—you are calmed by its gradual
decay, its slow return to the earth.

Andy

She was in a coma for three weeks. There were a million doctors and
specialists. They'd stroll into her room, stand at the foot of her bed,
glance at their watches, whisper in what sounded like Latin, and
then disappear without an explanation. I had to physically grab the
one that I assumed was in charge by the sleeve of his white jacket.
"What's going on?" I demanded. He had raised his note pad as if to
strike me with it, but relaxed when he saw the tears.

"No telling if she will come out of it, and if she does, no telling
what she will be like," he said.

All this *no telling* left me fearing the worst.

Elizabeth, Liza, L, you begin to abbreviate everything. You can't find the
energy to bother with formalities. Your head is filled with question marks
and exclamation points. You can't stop thinking about the concept of zero,
time and space. "I'm disappearing," you say, but no one seems to hear
you. You used to scream and kick at the walls. You were propelled by the

momentum of your anger, the residue of childhood tantrums, a core motiv-
ational force that drove you to the stage, but now you live in anticipation
of a memory—something that might explain this new and inexplicable
fascination with the perfection and mystery of the molecules vibrating
between and within. You are disappearing, but you are also expanding.

■

Agatha

When I first saw Liza, she was in the produce section of a grocery
store. Though it was August, she was wearing a turtleneck and pea
coat with the collar pulled up, a navy beret pulled over her ears. I
didn't really even notice her until we reached for the same tomato.
The extension of her arm revealed the blue and red ribbons of veins
between her coat sleeve and glove. Despite the pound of foundation
on her face, some of which was smeared on the rim of her hat and the
ends of her hair where it curled up on either side of her cheeks, she
had an exquisite profile. She let go of the tomato and quickly shuffled
away to squeeze and scrutinize the nectarines. I snuck another quick
look at her wrist to be sure and then, slowly approaching, I offered
her the tomato and apologized. As she walked away, I noticed a slight
limp in her gait, her legs swathed in winter leotards, her red rubber
boots squeaking as she hustled towards the checkout. I couldn't resist
the urge to follow her. "My name's Agatha," I said, giving her a quick
wink when she glanced back. She smiled and, even from that distance, I could see her mask crack as a line ran up the length of her
face on either side of her mouth.

■

You are in the matrix of time where seeds sprout, leaves grow, and fruit
ripens and decays. You spend long hours meditating on the impermanence
of nature. All other relationships feel like orbiting planets. Andy is out
there too. You recognize him, but aren't sure about the details. How long
had you been together? Do you love him? L is for Ludicrous performance

artist, but you can no longer relate to those exhibitionist impulses, the need for an audience to make your frustrations relevant is gone. You no longer want to build a body of work out of your body. You no longer wear army boots. You don't voice your opinions loudly in crowded bistros. You no longer feel compelled to leave a footprint in dry cement. All you want is to know who you are, who you are becoming. But you are forced to figure out this mess, in the wake of a public catastrophe that brought the audience to their feet. The ambulance lights casting a red intermittent glow through the emergency exit behind the stage while fingers typed out words like "electrifying," "shocking," and "transcendent," into the tweetosphere. The critics loved you, but you see it now: all your performances were little more than metaphorical screams, theatrical expressions of your need to be heard, complaints disguised as art.

Andy

I never really did get used to Liza's tendency to go about her day without any clothes on: naked cooking, although she wore an apron when frying anything in the wok; naked dishwashing—little soap bubbles popping on her eyelashes; naked television watching; naked discussions about the latest installations at the Guggenheim; and even naked violin playing—though I admit the combination of Tchaikovsky and the rise and fall of her breasts as she drew the bow across the strings took my breath away. Naked, naked, naked, she was always naked, and so I really appreciated it when she would concede to putting on a lacy little thing when we had sex. The divine Ms. L.

But as soon as she got home from the hospital, she put on a sweater, pulled the curtains closed, and unplugged all the lamps. She grew quiet. There was a time when you could set her off by simply leaving the toilet seat up, but she had become a whisper of herself, a shadow. Oh, and she became obsessed with fruit.

To say I was a little worried would be putting it mildly, but when she said she wasn't ever going to perform again—I mean what else can you do with an MFA?—I suggested she come work at the paint store.

■

Agatha

I love the human form—bone, muscle, the detail of skin. Light is the key. Throughout a career that has primarily focussed on portraiture, I have attempted to get at the soul of every subject I have shot, but Liza, well, you have to understand that what made Liza so special was that her soul was already exposed. All I had to do was point the camera and that was it. Capturing the miracle of her was more journalism than art.

I caught up to her out in the parking lot. I simply followed the trail of plums and cherries that led to her VW. I didn't ask her any questions. I simply treated her as I would any subject I wanted to shoot. I looked her in the eye, gave her a list of references, and the conditions of the contract. I was actually surprised when she said yes, even more so when she offered to do it for free. I pulled a pen out of my pocket and handed her my grocery receipt to write her address on. The pen was sticky with the scent of fermenting peaches when she handed it back.

■

Your apartment is a mess. You feel claustrophobic. You look at the odds and ends—mannequins, antique furniture, the rocking horse, the shelf of wigs, the Annie Lennox albums—the remnants of your former life. You tear down the parachute pinned up across the ceiling; auction off your framed Georgia O'Keeffe prints, vintage barber chair, and heirloom pinball machine on eBay; take down your chili pepper lights; and leave the blender, the coffeemaker, and the microwave out in the alley for the Salvation Army pick-up. And then, with a little bit of space, you breathe in the emptiness and wonder how you are going to break it to Andy—you will no longer have sex with him and yet you have agreed to take off your clothes for the strange woman you met at the grocery store.

■

Andy

Liza wasn't home when Agatha showed up at the door. "I must be a little bit early," she said, handing me a silver case and a tripod. Liza hadn't mentioned anything to me about a photoshoot, but Agatha assured me that she was expected so I helped her carry her camera equipment up the three flights of stairs.

It was just like Liza to be late, she was always late these days. Next thing I knew, I was helping this stranger set up the lights, tape down the power cords, position the backdrop. And then, when all that was done, she handed me a green apple and told me to take off my shirt. She kept sighing and shaking her head as she made subtle adjustments to the camera and the tripod. She was talking the whole time, going on about light absorption and the dark fabric of my jeans.

Several minutes later, I was standing there naked while she shot a roll and a half of film dedicated to the birthmark on my hip. I felt scrutinized and fragmented.

"It looks like a vagina," she said.

Agatha was long gone by the time Liza got home.

■

You wonder if there is any emotion left in you, it's hard to tell through eyes that see everything as if for the first time. You sift through the reviews of your work and wonder who that woman was. You search for the anger, but all you find is confusion, a vague sense of sadness. You search your mind, but you have nothing to say. You are communicating post-verbally now. Your need to be heard is now eclipsed by the feeling that there is nothing left to hear. You are fading, slowly disappearing, like a diagram in a second-hand copy of Gray's Anatomy.

You don't accept Andy's invitation to come work at the paint store he manages, you just show up one morning in a dirty pair of overalls.

He puts you to work in the stockroom where you spend a couple hours studying the paint-swatch colours.

■

Andy

She shows up late for work, mixes colours wrong every time, can't seem to follow the recipe for Sunflower Surrender or Lighthouse Blue, and yet I notice that the customers are satisfied, excitedly so. "That's the colour that I had in mind," they say. "I couldn't find the swatch that I was looking for, but that's it." Bruce and Gary take credit for it on the floor. She leaves the store with spots of paint on her face. She looks good in yellow, I think, a rather uplifting contrast to the blue of her indifference.

■

When Agatha arrives, she insists on paying you. But she wants more for her money. You stand there nervously, surrounded by umbrellas and lights, electrical wires coming out of a large, grey box running thick currents from the wall. Agatha leans in close and whispers reassuring words into your ear, gently licks your earlobe, and then twists the lid off a bottle of Grand Marnier. You sip and then drop your shoulders, sip again and uncork your legs, hold out the mug for more, and begin to hum along to the Chet Baker CD. Agatha grabs a camera and snaps the shutter randomly for a few minutes. She then drags the loveseat into view and gently pushes you down onto the couch, but you do not completely relax until you bite into a bruised apple. Agatha peers through the lens of the Leica. "Okay," she says. "Let's see some skin."

■

Andy

I couldn't believe it when I found the two of them on the couch laughing, Agatha wrapped in a towel and Liza in a bathrobe, leaning forward with her breasts showing. There were cherries, orange peel, mangoes, and an empty bottle of liquor on the coffee table. The floor was stained and sticky, littered with cherry seeds, peach pits, grape stems. Agatha gave me a cold look as if my presence meant the party was over. It was an awkward moment, but I had been witness to plenty of those before. Liza was an actress after all and the script often demanded that she compromise her better self.

■

Were you happy before? Are you happy now? You think about how excit-ing it was being photographed, like sharing a secret, admitting to a great big lie, exposing the florettes of milk glands blooming from your nipples, your face flushed with embarrassment and excitement. You remember the charge running from your brain down through your body, sparks leaping from your tongue as Agatha kissed you. But it is already gone. There is no emotion attached to the memory. You think about hiring yourself out to be put on display at the museum.

■

Agatha

I never meant to hurt anyone. I mean, I'm not a homewrecker. I just don't have much sympathy for men. Let's just say, I appreciate Lilith more than Eve, and no, I don't sleep with all my clients but then, well, L was different than anyone I had shot before. Never mind the obvious phenomenon of her body, she had a saintly quality about her, as if she was juggling simultaneous realities, conversing with angels. Just being in her presence did something to you; it slowed you down, made you move closer to whatever you were doing. And yet, in the end, all I wanted was to capture that magic. I mean, she was actually clinically dead for a while.

■

Andy

I was the one who spent those nights at her side in the hospital, paid those exorbitant overnight parking fees, filled her room with calla lilies, arranged the junk that friends and family felt obligated to buy from the gift shop in the lobby. I was the one who read to her each night from *A Deconstruction of Postmodernism*, underlining passages with a pencil whenever she twitched a finger or raised an eyebrow. I was the one who was there when she awoke.

Agatha, rotten apple, Agatha. She's a snake.

■

You remember his face. It was the first thing you saw when you woke up. He was crying and then you started crying too. And as you raised yourself up onto your elbows, you mistook the restraint of the tubes up your nose, the intravenous in your arm, and the apparatus over your mouth for the gentle tug of the deep comfort from which you were emerging. And when your eyes focussed, you could make out the eggshell walls reflecting the blue hue of fluorescent brightness, the distant sound of a doctor being paged, and you realized that you were crying, not because you were alive, but because you were not dead.

■

Andy

Liza was sitting on the toilet with the door open. "I have a question," she said.

"Shoot," I answered, clapping my hands at a cluster of fruit flies hovering over the kitchen sink.

"When did you move in?"

"When you were in the hospital," I said.

I heard her sigh and after a moment or two, the toilet flushed.

"I felt that it would be easier for us this way," I continued.

She stepped into the kitchen, her silk robe with dragons embroidered across the front hung open. Her ribs were slightly visible through the milky softness of her skin. "The only reason I was going out with you was because I was comfortable with you in bed."

Agatha stuck her head around the corner and I could see by her exposed collarbone that she was still not dressed. "I still have a roll of film left," she said.

I glanced at the mess on the table, the rinds of watermelon, the sticky seeds, and puddles of juice.

"I wasn't the one who plugged in the toaster," I said.

And then she asked me to leave.

■

You sit at the table and stare at the fruit you have arranged in front of you—an orange, a green apple, a peach, a bunch of blueberries, and a tomato. You break a wedge of orange apart and bite into a berry, split the seeds of an apple, and marvel at the micro perfection of each detail. You can see the colours—blue, red, orange—juice running through your veins. And you know that time is running out.

■

Andy
When I dropped by to pick up the last of my things, I found Agatha sitting on the kitchen floor with her face buried in her hands. It seemed strange to see her like that, emotional, vulnerable. She didn't look at me, but pushed the photos in front of her in my direction.

"Where's Liza?" I said.

"She's gone."

I stuck my head in the living room, peered behind the closet curtain, checked the bedroom. "Gone where?"

"Gone. Just gone," Agatha said. "There's no sign of her in any of the photographs."

I ran to the bathroom door. I could still hear Agatha around the corner repeating the words "she's gone, she's gone," as I pushed the door open and turned on the light. But there was nothing there but a pair of rubber boots in front of the sink.

The floor is slippery with pulp, fruit flies hover in slow, lazy circles, and you know that what you are seeing is not a memory, but right there in front of you—the stage of your final performance. You slip on your rubber boots and push open the bathroom door. The tub is a compost heap of rotting fruit. You empty the contents of the medicine cabinet into a glass and fill it with water. You pause a moment and, as you stare at yourself in the mirror, you appreciate the phenomenon of your exquisite transparency—your teeth in a sinister smile through the bluish hue of your lips; each eye, a round ball behind the crepe of your lids; your tear ducts, reddish seeds on either side of the bridge of your nose; honeycomb lymph nodes along your jawline; blue and red blood vessels running up your temples; a decomposing body. You pucker up and trace the soft curve of each lip with 'mackintosh red' lipstick. And then a tear falls and little sparks bounce across your cheek as you raise the glass of half-dissolved pills to your lips. You smile as you drink, knowing that when the curtain closes, you will have finally left your mark: a red smudge on the edge of an empty cup.

RED

Shards of bark and wood chips nipped and bit at my skin like black flies as I brutally hacked a rough V into the trunk of a sixty-foot-tall white pine. The dull blade and the clumsiness of each swing added a degree of frustration that turned my little tantrum into a full-blown manic episode. I could hear Lance's voice yelling at me to stop, receding into the forest. The blood in my veins boiling with a feverish anger.

Eventually, exhaustion set in, my arms grew weak from chopping, and I could hear Lance giving me what was clearly a final warning. "Last chance, Jardine." I fell to my knees and raised the hatchet to take one last swing. When Lance's foot connected solidly with my hand, the hatchet went spiralling into the flames of the campfire.

While our friendship was built on a series of ongoing insults and transgressions, this was the first time that I was so angry with him that the world became a carnelian blur.

"What is wrong with you?"

Lance was shouting now.

Blood, frustration, and guilt gave way to a sobering flush of embarrassment and pain. "I think my hand's broken," I said.

Lance's eyes went to the hatchet. The handle burst into flames.

"You're lucky that fucking thing landed in the fire or I'd be hanging your dumb scalp on my lodge pole right now."

I was just about to mention that remarks like that serve no purpose other than to perpetuate racial stereotypes when the tree I had so fervently attacked began to groan in the wind.

■

Archie Stansfeld Belaney was born in Hastings, Sussex, England, the product of a dubious marriage between his father and his father's sister-in-law. Archie was then abandoned when his parents ran off to America, leaving Archie to be raised under the harsh discipline of his two aunts. The scandalous nature of his beginnings would shape the mischievous and unpredictable course of Archie's life.

■

I was going to say that it all started with the imposter Wa-Sha-Quon-Asin, otherwise known as Grey Owl, but really, it began with another British author, T.H. White, and his book, *The Once and Future King*. We were in grade 8 and Lance clearly hadn't done the assigned reading because when I called him Sir Lancelot, he took what I intended as a witty play on his name to be an insult to his cultural heritage. He grabbed me by the hair, slammed me into the metal locker, and shoved me to the floor. The two swift kicks that followed left a red welt on my ribs. And then, just as quickly as the attack began, Lance took a step backwards. "Don't ever refer to me as a fictional character from the literature of a colonial empire again," he said. "I am Anishinaabe. A descendant of the original peoples of Canada."

For a second, it looked like he was going to cry, but as soon as I blinked, a look of anger and defiance returned to his face. As I watched him walk away, the humiliation of my public thrashing—there were several people watching the incident play out—gave way to a montage of images: teepees, buffalo on the plain, tomahawks, bows and arrows.

I spent lunch break on my own, nursing my wounded pride, while at the same time adrift in a state of curiosity and wonder. I had never met a real Indian before and, while the violence of this encounter was in line with the fierce, cruel, and wild warriors I had seen on television, the thing that stood out to me was the momentary hint of vulnerability I saw in Lance's eyes. I was reminded of the crying Indian from the *Keep America Beautiful* ads, which I made the mistake of mentioning to Lance the next day in the boys' washroom. He responded with another violent assault. My blond hair was spared this time on account of the baseball cap I was wearing, which Lance hung onto as he delivered a couple more solid kicks to my stomach. I was sitting on the floor next to the stink of a urinal when he told me that the actor in the ridiculous commercial that I had referred to was not Indian and that if I insulted him one more time, I'd wish I was back in England "sipping tea and eating crumpets with the goddamn queen."

Even though I was humiliated and confused, I was able to recognize that both violent attacks were provoked by, good intentions or not, displays of my ignorance.

▪

As a child, Archie was fascinated with the mythology and romance of the Canadian Indian. He ravenously read books and played the role of the "noble savage" with childhood friends. He was a distracted student and, despite the constant disciplinary measures of the School Master, he spent most of his youth dreaming of the Canadian wilderness. When Archie was eighteen, he was ready to test his knowledge and fortitude. He sold everything he had and left for Canada to pursue his dreams.

▪

I hobbled home from school that day wondering about my own identity. As an only child raised by a single parent, I had always felt rootless and insecure. I never knew my father—all I had was a photo of him taken by my mother at a party shortly after they first met. He was drunk, a beer in each hand, and he had a glazed look in his eyes. What I did know was that my mother was born and raised in Glasgow. She still had a bit of an accent, but aside from the odd reference to her childhood, she never really spoke about what being

Scottish was like. When I asked her about our ancestry, she told me that, thanks to my namesake, I was entitled to wear the tartan of the Jardine clan if I so desired. "But then you'd have to start eating haggis and learn to play the bagpipes," she said. I smiled and she laughed until I asked her about my father. "He was from Alberta and his ancestry, if you care to know, could be traced back to the gates of Hades." Beyond that, she knew nothing about him. "He was a scoundrel," she added, "but the long and short of it is, *you* are, *we* are, all Canadians."

I don't know why that made me feel so disappointed, but it did. "What," I asked, "did being Canadian mean?"

After the maple syrup, Mounties, and hockey clichés, we found ourselves in a silence of uncertainty.

I had hoped that I could go to school the next day and make some kind of declaration, proud or otherwise, about who I was and so I badgered my mother with more questions about Scotland. When I saw Lance the next day in the hall, I stepped into his path. "I'm not from England," I said. "I'm Scottish and where I come from we wear *quilts* and we never back down from a fight." I knocked him to the ground with a quick shove and kicked him four times in the stomach. "Consider it a history lesson," I said.

I knew that I hurt him, but I had no idea whether he would acknowledge this round as mine or not, so I ran to my next class as fast as I could.

■

After a brief stint working in Toronto, Archie headed north where he met Bill Guppy, a seasoned bushman who introduced him to the wilderness and taught him how to trap, canoe, and throw an axe—the physical manifestation of an apprenticeship that began in his imagination as a child. He took to these survival skills with a great degree of enthusiasm and dedication and, before long, he was venturing out on long journeys into the bush on his own.

■

I did my best to avoid Lance for the remainder of the school year and spent the bulk of the summer in the library. I learned all I could about Scotland, its 790 islands, its monarchy, the historical significance of the bagpipes, the nuances of its whisky, but none of it seemed to resonate with me. I couldn't seem to connect with a place that, though it was my maternal homeland, was several thousand miles away.

When I started digging into my father's genealogy—my mother told me his last name was of French origin—I discovered that I was the great-great-grandson of Jean Clemente, a missionary who had come from France in 1796, bringing the "salvation of Christ to the heathens." He was one of thirty-nine passengers, a motley crew of Catholics, convicts, and charlatans hurling into the deep blue mystery of the Atlantic.

By mid-August, I had made my way over to the Canadian History section of the library, where I spent hours flipping through texts on Indigenous cultural artifacts, Native mythology, and spirit animals. When I eventually came across a book about European contact with Aboriginal Peoples, my heart sunk. Not only had Europeans taken land that did not belong to them, but they also brought smallpox and measles, which, by 1900, had played a role in reducing Indigenous populations by ninety percent. I pictured my great-great-grandfather painstakingly translating the bible into Iroquoian, a misanthrope motivated by a righteous corruption to infiltrate and convert, trading infected blankets for furs and souls. While I could hide behind my mother's name, my father's missionary blood still coursed through my veins.

■

Archie later found work doing odd jobs in Temagami, where he met and married an Ojibwa woman, Angele Egwuna. Angele and her family introduced Archie to the ways of Indian life and culture. He earnestly embraced these teachings as well, once again tapping into a discipline and fervour he had never applied in school. He practised the knowledge he absorbed with the tact and demeanour of someone born and raised in the wilds. Angele eventually bore him two daughters and taught him to speak Ojibwa. But Archie's transformative appetites led him to abandon his family when he fell in love with a Mohawk woman, Gertrude Bernard, whom he later named Anahareo.

When school began in September, I caught up with Lance as he cut through the hydro field. His sable hair was now just long enough to pull back in a ponytail, while mine was embarrassingly short thanks to my mother's cut three days before.

"Hey," I said.

"What the hell do you want, Jardine?"

"I want my baseball hat back."

"It's mine," he said. "I won it in battle."

"How about a trade?" I said.

When I offered him the Hudson's Bay blanket, I braced myself for the violence I was sure would follow, but Lance just stood there staring back at me. And then he smiled. "It's a hat, Jardine, not a beaver pelt."

I stood my ground.

"Look," he said, "that fucking hat, along with all the other sport franchises with Indian logos, is an insult."

The next thing I knew, his lecture on appropriation transformed into an argument about whether it was the campaign of the Christians or the economic influence of the fur trade that had the biggest impact on the traditional Native way of life. According to Lance, when it came to the past, our politicians and teachers clearly weren't interested in the truth. They were, he claimed, determined to ignore the willful slaughter of his ancestors—people he referred to as if they were still around. I pictured a bunch of old people sitting on the branches of a big tree. "Yeah, like a family tree," he agreed. While this image reminded me of the guilt I was feeling, I was also aware that the argument had become a discussion. By the time we got to school, Lance and I had somehow become friends.

■

After being hired by the government as a ranger, Archie and Anahareo moved to Saskatchewan, where he further developed the character and personification of his childhood dream. He stifled his accent, dyed his hair black, and rubbed herbs into his skin to darken the pigment. He manufactured a new history claiming to be born in Hermosilla, Mexico to Catherine Cochise of the Jicarilla Apaches and George MacNeill, a Scot who served as a scout in the Southwest Indian Wars. A crucial element of this well-mapped lie was to keep the origins of his fabrications as far away from the history he was trying to erase.

■

I discovered that fall that Lance didn't live in a teepee as I had fantasized. In fact, he lived in one of the nicer houses in the neighbourhood. His mother worked part-time at a department store in the ladies' shoe department and his father, a dentist, had short hair and thick, black-framed glasses that made him look less like an Indian than, well, the actor pretending to be an Indian in the television commercial. Lance's five-year-old sister, despite Halloween being two weeks away, was dressed in a Wonder Woman costume. I don't know what I was expecting, but dinner at the Longboat house was a real letdown until I saw the animals. They had two turtles, a fish tank, three cats, and a squirrel. Lance said the squirrel was blind. "If I set it free, it wouldn't survive an hour. And if I let it out of the cage, the little bastard chews on everything in sight."

"In sight," I repeated. "That's funny."

Lance stuck a baseball card through the little bars and the squirrel puffed up his tail and attacked it with zest. "I call him Casper," he said, "after my uncle." He paused a moment, watching the squirrel chew up Catfish Hunter's head. "They're both crazy," he said, "but my parents say a bit of crazy can be a good thing."

It turned out Lance went to visit his Uncle Casper for a sweat every fall.

"I'm going next weekend," he said. "You should come, Jardine."

"What's a sweat?"

"It's a purification ceremony," Lance said. "Like a sauna, but hotter."

I pictured a bunch of pink-skinned Scandinavian people lounging in a spa.

"It's serious business," he added. "It might do you some good."

I wasn't really sure what he meant by *serious business*, but when Lance told me Casper lived in a van and did some kind of work with inmates, I knew my mom would never let me go.

The next day, I caught my mother coming out of the bathroom. I was heading to school and she was heading to work. I told her that I had been invited to go camping with Lance's family. I knew it was a lie, but I reasoned it out by telling myself that *sometimes a bit of crazy can be a good thing*. It wasn't until she said yes that I realized how nervous I was.

■

Anahareo tolerated Archie's talents and turbulences for nearly twelve years and supported his transformation both in his identity and in his philosophy. She was a strong-willed woman who influenced his views on the cruel elements of trapping and the environmental impact on a diminishing wilderness. Her traditional skills of beadwork and tanning leather outfitted Archie, who, by the late 1920s, adopted his Ojibwa name Wa-Sha-Quon-Asin—He Who Flies By Night—Grey Owl.

Though I was excited at the prospect of sleeping under the stars, chopping wood, and hunting for our food, I'd never been camping in my whole life and the further the Greyhound bus got from the city, the more anxious I felt.

Lance punched me hard in the arm. "You need to relax," he said. "You are going to have an encounter with Mother Nature. It's beautiful where we're going. There's moose and bear and water and trees. All you really need to worry about is how you're going to get the luggage you brought into the bush."

When we got off the bus, I heaved my suitcase over to the side of the road where Lance took a seat on his backpack and stuck his thumb out at a passing car. "My uncle is going to get a real kick out of you."

Lance chewed on a piece of red licorice while I practised throwing his hatchet at a highway sign. It was almost dusk when a car finally stopped to pick us up. The driver was a patient guy because it took several minutes for me to find the hatchet in the tall, yellow grass.

We were dropped off about twenty minutes down the road. Aside from the billboard advertising a local car dealership, there was nothing around us but the highway with forest on either side. The sun was behind the tree line.

"Now what?" I said, as the dust from the car that dropped us off settled on the shoulder of the road.

Lance heaved his backpack onto his shoulders. "Follow me," he said.

A few yards back, there was a rutted track that led into the trees. As soon as we entered the shade of the forest, I had the sense that I was being followed. I walked behind Lance, cursing and swearing for what seemed like a hundred miles.

The trail, or so Lance called it, eventually led to a clearing where a small fire turning to coals illuminated an old, beat-up trailer with its roof covered in tree branches. I put down the suitcase and tried to get the blood circulating back into my sore arm. Lance grabbed a stick, turned the coals, threw a couple pieces of wood over them, and then walked over to the trailer. He knocked, waited a moment for a response, and then pulled the door open. I followed him in.

The whole trailer was full of books. The kitchen counter and cupboards were piled high, even the fridge, which had its door removed, had stacks of paperbacks lining the shelves. A narrow trail just wide enough to squeeze through led to a bunk with a sheepskin cover tucked in at the edges. Lance grabbed my arm, "He's not here. We should wait outside."

We had been sitting on a pair of beat-up lawn chairs for about a half hour staring at the fire, when Lance gave me a nudge with his elbow and then stood up. The old man came into the clearing, pushing a wheelbarrow full of big, smooth stones. He gave Lance a warm hug and then started placing the stones around the fire. He didn't acknowledge me until the wheelbarrow was empty. "Who's this?" Casper said, tapping me on the chest with the burnt tip of the stick Lance had used on the coals. I resisted the temptation to wipe at the black smudge left on my shirt and shot Lance a dirty look.

"His name is Tom Jardine. He's from the unicorn clan."

The sound that came out of Casper's mouth was not immediately recognizable as a laugh. In fact, it sounded more like a coughing fit and, if it weren't for the sparkle in his eyes, I might of thought he was about to keel over.

After straightening himself out, he poked me with the stick again. "If you're gonna hang around," he said, "you gotta do the work."

A moment later, he was in his trailer rummaging about. I turned to Lance, who was nonchalantly chewing on another piece of licorice.

"You didn't tell him I was coming, did you?"

Lance turned to the fire. "He probably would have said no."

When Casper came back out of the trailer, he tossed a book at me, which, as it caught me by surprise, fluttered through the air, hit me in the chest, and then fell to the ground. "Read that," he said.

I fanned the pages and then turned the cover towards the fire-light, *Pilgrims of the Wild*, the story of Grey Owl.

"I want it back before you go," he said. "I'm running out of toilet paper."

■

Anahareo's influence was instrumental in Grey Owl's further transform-ation from guide and trapper to writer, filmmaker, and lecturer. Grey Owl, who had at this point completely reinvented himself, wrote five books, numerous magazine articles, and produced several films. He toured Canada, the States, and England, often drunk and in full Indian regalia, preaching the gospel of preservation. "A time will come," he prophesied, "when a well-taken photograph will be a greater test of a good hunter than the possession of a head or a hide."

■

Lance and I spent the next half hour setting up a mouldy, canvas tent that Casper had dragged out of his trailer. We stayed up reading by flashlight and, despite the strange greeting, I felt seduced by a sense of adventure and excitement, that is, until the light went out. I lay awake most of the night frozen in fear by the sounds of the creatures sniffing and snorting around our tent. Lance assured me that they were only raccoons, but my imagination couldn't be satiated by the image of something so familiar. "Sounds more like a grizzly bear," I told him. It wasn't until Lance yanked open the fly and pointed his flashlight out into the darkness that I loosened my grip on the handle of the hatchet.

Casper disappeared into the bush the next morning, leaving us with enough chores to keep us busy all day. While we were strolling through the forest gathering bows of cedar, Lance pointed out the trees that were indigenous to Canada and others that were imported from Europe. "You can tell by the bark and the leaves," he said.

I was struck by the realization that colonization had done its work here in the forest as well.

Later that day, as we hitchhiked into town to bum money for what Lance called *ceremonial tobacco*, Lance interrupted our conversation to identify another tree. "Look," he said. "There's your grandmother."

He was pointing at a rotting Scotch pine. I hit him hard in the ribs and bolted to avoid the punch that would surely follow, but when Lance caught up with me, he reached out and cuffed my forehead with the palm of his hand.

"What was that?" I said, trying to catch my breath.

"A coup," he said. "It's an act of bravery."

I finished *Pilgrims of the Wild* on the second night. The book left me feeling ambivalent. Like Iron Eyes Cody, Grey Owl was a fraud and I couldn't help feeling like a fraud as well. I hadn't told Lance that I came from a line of people who, once upon a time, contributed to the annihilation of his ancestors. I closed the book, but I kept the flashlight on.

"Go to sleep, Jardine," Lance finally said. "The sweat starts at sunrise."

▪

Grey Owl became a celebrity, a cultural icon whose biography to this day stimulates a recursive mixture of awe and distaste. He was many things. He manufactured his identity, he abandoned his history, he fought authentically for the preservation of the wilderness. He was a scoundrel.

▪

It was still dark when Casper woke us up. As I stumbled about, I saw that someone was tending the fire, a featureless shape that seemed to move as if it were part of the darkness itself. I was cold, hungry, and delirious, and, even though I had no idea what I was getting myself into, the moment we crawled into the sweat lodge, it was clear to me that my whole life had been leading to this moment. The ceremony began with several offerings and prayers, during which Casper's voice possessed a quiet authority that seemed to command the seriousness that Lance had reminded me about several times. Each time Casper dropped a ladle of water onto the stones, the heat intensified and I sank closer to the ground. The rocks hissed, the steam rose, and my lungs burned. Eventually, the dark outline of Lance and Casper vanished and I could feel myself withdraw into a slow and overwhelming surrender. Time began to tumble and if it weren't for the coolness of the earth, I wouldn't have known which way was up. I could feel my heart begin to race and then slow to the point that I wondered if it had stopped. Just as I was about to call out to Casper, to tell him that I had had enough, I noticed that something was moving in the earth in front me. I had the sense that I had drifted into an altered state, that I had somehow become disconnected from the rules of rationality and, like the mighty and sorrowful Jack pine in Grey Owl's book, I watched as a tree sprouted from the seed of a pinecone. As the tree grew into the darkness above, its roots broke out of the ground and entwined themselves around my ankles. I began to panic and once again I wanted to call out, but as soon as I opened my mouth, my father appeared and handed me an axe.

■

Despite the thoroughness of Archie's transformation from English immigrant to Apache conservationist, the reality of his past, the life he had created, and the uncertainty of his future coalesced into a turbulence that ultimately inspired him to drink away his anxiety of being discovered. By this point, Archie had the reputation of knowing the woods as well as he knew the bottom of a whisky bottle.

■

I had no memory after that. I can't be sure if I crawled out of the sweat lodge on my own or if my unconscious body was dragged out into the light. When I opened my eyes, Casper was sitting beside me. "Drink this water," he said, "and when you leave, take the spirit with you."

At some point during the long stretch of time that I spent staring into the fire, Casper climbed into his van and left without a word. I felt weak and troubled, and, though I wanted to talk to Lance, tell him what I had experienced, I couldn't seem to keep track of his movement around the camp. I turned my attention back to the fire and, after drifting in and out of another spell, I reminded myself to drink more water. As I got up and staggered over to the Coleman, I spotted Lance's hatchet. The next thing I knew, I was going berserk on the tree.

Although many academics and Indians knew Archie was a fraud, he managed to fool thousands of people, including government officials, King George VI, and The New York Times. He died of pneumonia in 1938 at the age of 49, just prior to being exposed by a newspaper that had withheld the truth of his identity for three years.

I slept by the fire that night in the dirt. In the morning, Lance gave me a kick and, when I sat up, he handed me a cup of hot tea. "How's your hand?" he asked.

I made a fist and then extended my swollen middle finger. "It hurts like hell," I said, "but it seems to work fine."

Lance turned to the sixty-foot white pine and fixed his gaze on the brutal wound I had made in its trunk. "That tree will have to come down now," he said. "Otherwise it might fall on Casper's trailer in the next storm."

I felt terrible. "How old do you think it is?"

"I don't know, but it's an elder for sure."

It dawned on me then that I had damaged something that was important to both of us. "I'm sorry," I said.

Lance kicked at the ground with the toe of his shoe. "An apology is a good start," he said. "But there's more work to be done."

The tree seemed to sigh and then creak as a breeze high over our heads pushed it gently to the east.

When Lance extended his hand to help me up, I realized that we were no longer quarrelling about the past; instead, we were talking about the future.

LOW AND AWAY

My mother used to say that dog was crazy—a menace to the neighbourhood. Don't know where it came from, it was just there one day, scratching at its haunches on the neighbour's front lawn. Spent the nights sleeping under the porch, but as soon as the sun came up, it started making a racket, running like the devil down that stretch of torn-up lawn, barking and howling at everything that passed. Nearly gave old man Turner down the road a heart attack. He passes on the other side of the road now. Carries a long stick whenever he goes to pick up his mail.

My mom said that that dog was just like my father—a son of a bitch mix of all the worst breeds, angry at the world and ugly as hell. The cops, who had paid a visit to the Nelsons' on more than one occasion, said there was nothing they could do as long as the dog stayed on the property. And that was the strange thing about it, for all its craziness, that dog acted like it had an invisible rope tied around its neck. Never saw it once step a foot off the lawn. I suppose my dad and the dog were similar in that department too—since the accident, my dad had never been off the property either. The wheelchair, the drinking, and the sports channel pretty much defined his existence. Sometimes he didn't even bother getting dressed. He'd spend the whole day hanging around in his pyjamas, which had burn holes all over them from the cigarettes he put out on his skinny legs. "It's the only goddamn thing they're good for," he said once. I did my best to stay out of the way, both my dad's and the dog's. My mom, on the other hand, she was always getting barked at.

I used to have a little book I kept in my pocket. Used it to keep track of things. How many fights they had, who got the better of who—with my father in the chair, my mom had some advantages, but he was strong and still had a pretty good arm. Things got so bad that I got in the habit of staying in bed each morning for a minute or two, just listening to see what kind of a mood my dad was in, whether he was drinking, whether the cable subscription had been paid, whether it was safe to leave my room. Kept dates and notes on those stats too. I was late for school 1.3 times per week in the month of September. I joined a bunch of after-school clubs so I had an excuse to not be around until my mom was home from work. On days where I didn't have chess, choir practice, badminton, or detention, I'd go to the library, which was where I was coming home from on the night I found my mom crying on the porch.

The dog started making a racket as soon as he heard the tires of my bike on the gravel. I didn't slow down until I got to our driveway, where I dismounted because the car, which was on an angle, meant I had to pick up my bike to get it past the tight space between the car's front fender and the hedge. I locked up to the drainpipe and, as I headed for the front porch, I could see that the only light inside the house was coming from the television in the living room.

I didn't see my mom sitting there on the step until she spoke.

"Someone should put the bastard out of his misery," she said.

As she took a drag from her cigarette, the red glow was bright enough that I could see the dark streaks of the tears she had wiped at on her cheeks .

"Some things would be better off dead."

I looked over at the neighbour's yard, the torn-up, shit-covered lawn, and then at the front door of our own house, the tear in the screen, the flickering blue light illuminating the beer can lying on the front hall floor.

"Sorry I'm late," I lied.

"I was worried. Where have you been?"

"The library," I said holding the book up. "It's for a history assignment."

"What is it?"

"It's about Paris before the first World War."

She looked up at the sky, took a drag, and blew a smoke ring into the darkness. "*La belle époque.*"

I stood there for a moment, waiting, and when it became obvious that she wasn't going to elaborate, I stepped past her and opened the screen door.

"I wouldn't go in there," she said.

I heard the sound of a beer being cracked open, the roar of a baseball stadium cheering a home run, my father cursing in response. I flicked on the porch light and stepped back outside.

My mom scooched over and patted the empty space on the step. As I sat down beside her, I saw the dark circle swelling under her eye. "I hate it when you cry," I said, "it means he's winning."

She wiped at her cheek and winced. "He wasn't always a prick you know—"

I knew the story. He was smart and handsome once, a talented prospect, had a 92-mph fastball, got a scholarship and everything, but he never made it to the pros—something about intangibles. He coached for a while in the Northern League, took the Winnipeg Goldeyes to the finals three seasons in a row, but they never won the Championship. There was even a time when he was determined to make me into a ballplayer, too. The batting box that he'd chalked on the shed door had long ago been washed away by the rain, but his incessant drilling was still there like a dark bruise in my memory. "Put your weight on your back foot," he'd yell. "Okay, now, 3 and 0, what do you think's coming?"

"Low and away," I'd answer hopefully.

Sometimes I was right, sometimes I was wrong, and even though I only ever managed to squib a grounder, which usually went foul, I'd imagine the ball arcing high into the air as it travelled off into the blue sky, far beyond the horizon of trees to disappear in the clouds, never to be seen again.

He finished each practice with a fastball that came high and inside, a pitch that, even when anticipated, froze me on the spot and left a painful welt on my ribs. The intangibles put an end to my dad's ball career and the tree he drove into on his way home from a shift at the mill put an end to what was left of his hopes and dreams.

As my mother wrapped up the latest version of my father's story, we sat there for a moment staring up into the star-filled sky together. When she spoke again, her voice sounded far away. "Mrs. Nelson next door was from France. Did you know that?"

I shrugged.

"Maddy Nelson used to be Madeline Tremblay before she got married."

I looked over at the Nelsons' place. The light from the living room window illuminated the decrepit porch where the crazy dog was scratching manically at its flea-bitten ribs. Considering the general mess of the place, it was hard to imagine that there ever was a Maddy Nelson. The rose-coloured curtains and dusty sheers had been replaced with a tattered Canadian flag, the screen door clanged and rattled every time a little breeze came up, and the garden was little more than an overgrown mess of weeds and dog shit.

My mom lit a cigarette off the one she had been smoking and then just sat there with one in each hand. "Maddy sent me a postcard," she said. "After she left."

A loud crash in the house made my mom's shoulders tense, as if she was waiting for something to hit her. Lightning and thunder in reverse. Another tear rolled down her cheek. She turned back to the dark sky, her face obscured momentarily by the cloud of blue smoke she exhaled through her nostrils. "You'll never guess what it said."

"Guess what, what said?"

"The postcard…with the Eiffel Tower on it."

I shrugged again.

It was then that my mother noticed that she was holding two cigarettes. She flicked the butt of the burned-down one onto the hood of my dad's Buick. I watched it roll off the fender and come to rest on the driveway, next to the car's flat tire.

"The only words she wrote on the postcard were: *Plan B.* No greetings, no itinerary, just *Plan B.*"

"What does that mean?" I asked.

She paused and glanced over at the Nelsons' place. "It's what you do when Plan A turns to shit..."

We sat there for a while, watching the neighbour's dog chew on the piece of splintered lattice it had torn away from the skirting around the Nelsons' porch.

"I'm hungry," I said.

My mom glanced back at the door. My dad's nightly drunken ritual of slamming his wheelchair into things and cursing at the television was underway. "Stay here," she said. She dropped her half-smoked cigarette on the step and got up. As she headed for the door, I heard the ping of a moth crashing into the exposed light bulb. She didn't even try to stop the door from slamming when she stormed into the house.

When the fight began, I turned my attention to the Nelsons' front lawn. The dog had a way of blending into the shadows and dirt, but at that moment he was visible, napping in the glow of the light coming out of the Nelsons' front window. I remember thinking how different he looked curled up like that. You could almost imagine cuddling up with him and giving him a scratch under the chin.

Half an hour later, my mom came limping down the hall, lugging a suitcase. As she shoved the screen door open, a beer can hit the wall behind her. She didn't stop until she had made it down to the walk that led to the curb. She stood there for a long moment, staring back at the door, before she finally put the suitcase down, lit a cigarette, and tossed the match on the grass.

"Pack a bag," she said.

I kept my eyes on the burning match and stared at it until it went out. A siren wailed off in the distance. I didn't know I was holding my breath until she spoke again.

"It'll be different this time," she said.

When I looked at her, she took a long drag off her cigarette and tried to smile.

I knew the routine: the room at the shelter, counselling, the sharing circles, the problem-solving and self-esteem workshops, the tears, the promises. And then, after a few weeks, she'd soften and call to see how he was doing and before you knew it, we'd be back here. It would be fine for a week or two, and then, like clockwork, a new season would begin. "I'm staying," I said.

She dropped her cigarette, crushed it under her foot, and picked up the suitcase. When she got to the sidewalk, she paused. "You sure?"

I nodded.

She took another few steps and turned around again. "I'll write you," she said. "I'll send you a postcard."

■

I spent a lot of time on the front porch over the next couple of weeks as my father raged against my mother's leaving. He'd drink himself into a state of jovial, devil-may-care obliviousness, which would sometimes decline into sentimental blubbering before amping up into a violent and cold anger. During the occasional reprieve when my father was too tired and sick to get himself in a lather, we'd sit by the window, staring out at the street, both of us waiting for a cab to pull up and drop my mother off.

When a month passed, I began to wonder if she had actually managed to escape. I checked the mail, sorting through the bills and junk for a picture of something French. I imagined my mom and Madeline Tremblay sitting in a café, sipping glasses of wine. I missed her terribly, but I preferred the idea of never seeing her again to the beatings she would take if she came home.

By early November, the days had gotten shorter, the nights were getting cold, and my dad launched into one of his experimentations with sobriety. During this spell, he'd drift back and forth between woeful self-pity and sunny ideas about the future. He'd apologize, make a million promises, and of course he'd get the Willie Nelson record out.

"This was her favourite record," he said, staring down at the album cover.

He was lying. I knew that. All the things that she cared about were either with her in France or at the bottom of the stairs in the basement where my dad had thrown them when she left.

I had just put on my shoes and was about to head out to school when the last song on the album ended.

"Hey," he said, "stay home today. Keep your old man company."

"I got a test," I lied.

I could see his knuckles whiten as he gripped the armrests on his chair, but then he took a deep breath and closed his eyes, as if he was fighting some uncontrollable urge. I had my hand on the door when he called out. His voice was much louder now. I hesitantly took a few steps back down the hall to the living room.

"Do me a favour," he said, "and flip the record before you go."

I came home from school that day to find my dad on the phone in the kitchen placing an order. I kept my shoes on. I knew the routine. Mr. Abernathy would have the beer waiting by the time I got to the liquor store. Then I'd swing by the Beckers' next door for a lottery ticket and cigarettes before heading over to the IGA for groceries. My dad tossed four twenties on the table and pointed at the plastic garbage bags filled with dented beer cans next to the fridge. When I went to pick up the money on the table, I saw the envelope. There was no mistaking her handwriting. I felt my own two hands clench into tight fists.

"Your mother's coming home tomorrow," he said. "I want this place cleaned up when you get back."

It wasn't until I was on my way home, dead centre in the stretch of sidewalk that spanned the length of the Nelsons' wide yard, when the dog scuttled out from under the porch. There was a brief pause while we made eye contact, and then, as if the dog suddenly remembered that it was nuts, it came tearing across the lawn with the fury of hell in its eyes. The result of that terror triggered another moment of temporary paralysis and, by the time I managed to get my feet moving, I tripped over myself. I hit the sidewalk, the carton of cigarettes, the bread, the frozen dinners, and the cans of beer and soup spilled out of the bag I was carrying. I rolled over, expecting to see the dog lunging at my throat, but instead, it skidded to a halt, grass and dandelions splaying between its toes. The dog was close enough that I could smell its sour breath, see the rage in its bloodshot eyes as it tugged and lunged along the property's edge. As I got to my knees and gathered the beer and groceries, I had the sense that my mother was right. Somebody should put that animal out of its misery.

Later that night, my dad caught me in the kitchen. "Those cold-air molecules cost money," he said. We weren't allowed to have lights on in the house until it was completely dark outside for the same reason you had to make up your mind what you wanted out of the fridge before you opened it. I knew that, but the beer cans were making it hard to find the mustard bottle. He gave the fridge door a shove as he aimed the right tire of his wheelchair at my bare foot to emphasize the point. I was too slow.

"Who do you think is paying for all that wasted energy?"

It took all of my willpower to keep from crying.

"Sit down," he said.

He always made me sit down when he was going to give me hell because it made us the same height. I pulled the chair out from the table, and even though I could feel my crushed toes swelling, I stayed standing.

"Sit down," he said again.

His shoulders were drawn in and his voice, though measured,

now had an edge of holy terror in it. I knew I'd never make it to the safety of the front door, so I ran for the basement.

When I looked back up the stairs, my dad was silhouetted by the kitchen light. He was yelling at me, but the words blurred into an inarticulate bark of aggression and frustration. When he finally retreated, his path could be mapped by the violence he inflicted on the kitchen. I could hear the fridge door being slammed closed, the opening of a beer can, the sweep of his arm clearing the sandwich I was making on the counter onto the floor above me.

I had made an error. There was nothing in the basement but a milk crate full of my dad's old trophies, a pair of winter tires, golf clubs, a canvas bag full of baseball gear—bats, balls, gloves, a few caps, some dirty socks and cleats, and of course, all the stuff that my dad had thrown down there after my mother left.

He wasn't always a prick, my mother would say, he was once a talented prospect—had a 92-mph fast ball. I took out my notebook and made an entry. Two out, bottom of the ninth.

I don't know what time it was when I climbed the stairs and opened the door, but my dad was still there in the kitchen. He was barely conscious, his eyes red with anger and alcohol. When he focussed on the bat in my hands, he smiled.

The cleats I was wearing were a few sizes too big and the jersey smelled mouldy and rotten with a tinge of disappointment and regret. As I stepped past him, I shoved the armrest on his wheelchair, which sent him crashing into the cupboards behind him. His temper flared immediately, but when he came after me, the beer tucked between his legs stymied his drunken progress. I was halfway to the front door before he even made it out of the kitchen. Stolen base, I thought. I could hear him swearing, threatening to break my legs, his wheelchair banging into the wall as he pitched himself down the hall.

The moment I crashed through the front door onto the porch, the dog next door began to bark. I looked back at my dad snapping at the air. My legs trembled, but this time my fear gave way to a concise and determined plan. Plan B. I pulled the screen door open, stepped back into the house, and raised the baseball bat. Shoulders square, weight on the back foot. And while that crazy dog howled and raged, I knew what was coming: low and away. I made a quick adjustment and swung. I felt the solid thud of the wood connect and my eyes followed the trajectory of that ball arcing high into the air as it travelled off into the blue sky far beyond the horizon of trees to disappear in the clouds, never to be seen again.

HAMARTIA

Act One:

When the curtains part, I curtsy like a lady, bow like a gentleman, spit like the heathen I am. A conjurer of spells, a weaver of tales, I am a playwright whose tendencies lean towards the themes of Greek tragedy—love, loss, woeful heroes—the drama of my clichéd soul. The stories that I compose come from my breasts, my vulva, body memories scarred with scandals and deception. I have made a blood-stained career out of giving voice to the ghosts that haunt me, but lately, I'm not really sure where the theatre begins or ends, how much is performance, whether or not the blood is real.

If there ever was an appetite for theatre that concerns itself with repression, fear, and other misogynistic tendencies of his-story, the hunger for such things has waned. Times being what they are, the critics have not been kind. I have been accused of having an axe to grind, of being agenda driven, trauma obsessed, and bluntly brutal. But if my work has lost its subtlety, it is because the spirits I grapple with are aflame with anger and pain.

The trouble started when my husband vanished. Twenty years together and then, just like that, I woke up one morning and he was gone. He left me with a mortgage in receivership, an unpaid cable bill, and a garage full of empty beer cases, but I am not looking for sympathy. This is not a sad story, it is a tragedy and the sudden disappearance of my husband was little more than the inciting incident from which the downward spiral of this narrative manifested. I filed the missing persons report, as a good wife should, on the fifth day—he could have been off on a bender. The fact that he left without his pickup truck, without notifying his boss, and without his golf clubs couldn't be explained. And my failure to muster a single tear bothered colleagues, family, and the police, alike.

As soon as the investigation was made official, the company that had commissioned the script I was working on reneged on the contract. Rumours spread and my grant applications were rejected. By the end of the month, I couldn't even get my work staged on the Fringe circuit. But things really got out of hand when I was sitting in a café, reading the weekend paper, and I came across an article claiming that the state of theatre had been in decline since it had become politicized by the tyrannical and belligerent feminists of my artistic generation. The heat started in my chest and with each beat of my heart, it began to radiate through my body. Within seconds, my fingertips were tingling and the newspaper in my hands burst into flames. By the time the firetruck arrived, the cafe was dark with smoke and the sprinkler system had been activated.

The doctors at the medical institution where I was incarcerated for eighteen months insisted that both my decline as a playwright and my pyromaniacal tendencies were symptomatic of something called *delusional hysteria*, but they would never understand that there are forces at work that cannot be corralled by a label in the DSM. Nor could they comprehend that my husband's sudden departure was simply a matter of writing him out of existence. A sentence involving a shovel and the digging of a hole, and he was gone.

While the second-degree burns on my fingers healed, I endured the probings, the talk therapy, and the traumatic experiments they subjected me to and, in a pharmaceutically induced fog, I learned to distinguish that which is fancy from that which is real. But what I really learned was that being deemed fit to return to society was simply an improvisation, another role to be played. The moment I was home, I returned to my work. This, my latest production, a monologue as at this point I'm sure you are aware. I am the producer, the writer, the director, and the principal. And with the aid of a grant designated for creative types with "emotional disabilities," I stand before you on this stage. A single candle, a laptop, a spotlight, and a confession.

Act Two:
This scene begins with an addendum to the script. It is inspired by the heat presently smouldering in my core. I have known the source of it my whole life. It is the feverish anger of a woman born more than 700 years ago—a woman of exceptional intelligence and fortitude, who possessed the unfortunate habit of looking men right in the eye. It is the anger of a woman who spoke with confidence, who could read and write—qualities that inspired in the men of that dark age discomfort and sometimes outright outrage. Her journals were replete with baffling and intoxicating verse, celestial mappings, and blasphemous pagan concepts, which confirmed that she was in cahoots with Lucifer—how else could such qualities of the intellect be possessed by a woman who lived 200 miles from the nearest university or monastery?

The woman I speak of is more than a memory. She is an echo, one of 200,000 women executed by fire, raging against annihilation, her clenched fists engulfed in flames. And now that she has been remembered, it is too late for water; all that I can do is tell her story.

Angéle de la Barthe was a midwife, an herbalist, a healer. She knew a great deal about law, biology, and the night sky. She was called upon whenever someone was ill or a birth was imminent. She set fractured bones, cut umbilical cords, sutured wounds, and, on occasion, settled disputes over debts and other community grievances. She knew the Latin names of plants, was known to quote the Greeks, and, while her services were in demand, her eccentricities led to all manner of gossip and speculation.

Angéle always suspected that she was destined to burn, not because of any gift of clairvoyance, but because the searing heat radiating within her body was sometimes so strong that she felt it would one day consume her. According to her journals, she had, since her first menses, been afflicted with chronic fevers, the intensity of which she believed would do harm and injury to a lover. *Nothing can go inside of me*, she wrote. *Without proper diagnosis, I cannot treat this malady and, as long as the symptoms persist, I dare not risk subjecting another to this furnace.* Without the possibility of perhaps someday, all her suitors gave up eventually, even the women.

She lived quietly with this curse. When an episode was upon her, she slept with the windows open, went barefoot in the snow, leaving deep, steaming prints in her wake. She furnished her home with things made of steel, stone, clay, and glass—things that would not burst into flame when imagination and lust got the better of her. On the occasions when these fevers grew unbearable, she would fill a tub with ice, climb in, and fall asleep to the hiss of her cooling desire.

One night, with Mars gleaming tiny and red like the pupil of the devil in the sky, Angéle had a nightmare during which a beast entered her home through a window, climbed into her bed, and tore the clothes from her body. She fought with the will of her soul until she was overcome by a deep and numbing darkness. When she awoke in the morning, she found a man lying beside her, the general area of his pelvis, a black and bloody smouldering mess. Similar marks were discovered on her own body. She made a poultice of aloe, calendula, and comfrey, wrapped it to her groin, and dragged the dead man out into the woods where she buried him unceremoniously under a willow tree.

The assault turned Angéle into a recluse. She locked up her windows and door and never ventured into town again. She refused to act as moderator, nor could she be wooed with money or other pledges to practice midwifery. This self-imposed isolation coincided with a series of maleficent events. A drought hit, livestock were bloodied and wounded by an unknown predator, rats were spreading disease. The winds of those fearful times stirred the paranoid hearts of the townsmen. And then, on the eve of a new year, a farmer entered the town hall claiming to have seen Angéle on the roof of her cottage, baying at the moon. The tinderbox was dry and under such parched conditions, rumour became spark. A drunken militia was formed, and with pitchforks and hoes, they set out to put an end to the curse that had brought such havoc and destitution to the town.

Like Sappho, the verdict at the trial was, "she knows too much." In the fall of the year 1275, Angéle was tried, convicted, and sentenced to death by a mob of hysterical farmers. It is said that pages torn from the tragedies of Sophocles along with those of her forced confession were used as fuel for her incineration. As the pyre was lit, Angéle raised her head to the sky and cursed her audience—an execration that echoed from the amphitheatres of Athens to the sanitariums of Paris.

In death, Angéle found no rest. She returned transmigrationally every generation, once as a newborn in a small village in Tuscany—a miracle reinvented as myth hours later when the infant lit the sheets on fire with her breath. She appeared later during the British Raj in India as a twelve-year-old whose groom burst into flames on their wedding night. More recently, the fever of her incarnation emerged in the spirit of the poet Sylvia Plath, whose brilliance was tainted by mysterious visions of flaming spectres. Ms. Plath placed her head in her stove and turned on the gas.

It is this same unbearable affliction of heat that compels my thoughts towards annihilation—as I, too, have inherited Angéle's creative fevers, fevers that force me to compose my insomniatic monologues by the cool light of an open refrigerator door. I have endured the psychotropic manipulations of prescribed pharmacology, been interrogated, electrocuted, and lobotomized. The treatment for hauntings and reincarnation is clinical and abusive. But I have performed excavations of my own, which have led to this deeper and more accurate diagnosis. The remedy is simple: give voice to the spirit that possesses you.

As it is I who has resuscitated Angéle's tragic memory, it is my hand that must put her to rest. The only question is—what instrument of deliverance will be appropriate? Fire is the obvious choice, but I am a traditionalist and so I turn my mind to the Greeks. The plot is simple. All that is required is an audience, a hero, and the hero's death. In this case, we have a heroine, and anyone with an ounce of pagan blood might agree that the line between the stages of Athens, where countless hands drove knives deeply into the hearts of actors, and the real-life theatre of witch burnings, is drawn in blood. And so I choose the carving knife, point the tip of it to my stomach, cotton and dermis the only barrier. For a moment, I think that it would be easy: the will of the knife, to carve and slice through flesh, vibrating in my hands. But I catch myself when a vision of blood spilling onto the stage breaks the spell. My sympathy for the house custodian gets the better of me. I turn to the laptop and google alternatives. Not far down the page, I come across a suitable alternative. I add the recipe to the script: Secobarbital, sodium-9g, purified water-15ml, propylene glycol-10ml, dry gin-50ml, and one Greek olive—a more humane option to the mess of a knife or death by fire.

Whether it is real or theatre, in the end, tragedy always draws a crowd and tonight, this contemporary adaptation returns to its Classical origins and offers its audience that which it craves—a fall from grace and finally death—the only conclusion worthy of their hard-earned drachmas.

Which of course brings us to the Final Act.

I look out at the audience, faces expectant and focussed in the hot Athenian sun on a silence that has reverberated through the centuries. I imagine Angéle at my side, her hair aflame. I extinguish the candle, smile, and drink the poison.

When the authorities arrive, they will approach, not with pitchforks and guns, but with flashing lights and life-saving apparatus. But it will be too late. The atrocity has been remembered. And this time, it will not be forgotten.

The woman is perfected.
    Her dead
    Body wears the smile of accomplishment,
    The illusion of a Greek necessity.[1]

I swoon and collapse as dramatically as I can manage to the floor. And as the poison does its work, my heart explodes into flame. When I exhale, a thin line of smoke rises up into the lights and then vanishes.

The audience hesitates,
    and then,
    reluctantly applauds.

END NOTE:
1. Sylvia Plath, "Edge" from *Collected Poems*

HUNGRY GHOSTS

"If we don't leave, I'll have to kill him."

Duke's words echoed in my head as I shuffled down the driveway. His footprints ahead of me were marked by intermittent drops of red in the falling snow. We grabbed our stuff on the fly—the basketball; a roll of toilet paper, a portion of which my brother stuffed up his bleeding nose; two sleeping bags; a half pound of weed; and our dog, Biscuit, who fit without complaint into my backpack alongside a change of clothes and my squeegee gear. My brother was near the corner when I reached the end of the driveway. He always walked fast when he was wound up, like he was trying to leave his feelings behind. Chip off the old block. I took my time—wasn't in a hurry to get wherever the hell we were going—didn't even turn when I heard the old man raging at the front door. "You'll be back. Mark my words. You goddamn kids will be back!" He was too much of an asshole to bother putting on his shoes and come after us.

When I caught up with Duke at the bus station, he was holding two one-way tickets to Vancouver. His nose had stopped bleeding, but his chin had a red smudge on it.

"The rain's gonna suck," he said. "But at least we won't freeze to death."

We had half an hour to kill, so we put Biscuit on his lead and headed over to a parking lot across the street and smoked a joint. I leaned my head against the side of a dumpster. "Jesus Christ," I sighed, and at that moment, I felt a sense of hopelessness as I settled back into the need of my newly forming habits.

We arrived in Vancouver at seven in the morning on an unexpectedly sunny day. We needed money, so we started working the traffic outside the train station, a busy intersection with good, long reds. It was hit and miss as usual, but among the ornery bastards who told us to keep our filthy hands off their windshields, the kindness of strangers prevailed.

We met Samantha around noon. She'd been watching us for a while, leaning up against a mailbox smoking cigarettes, lighting one off the other. She walked right into traffic, completely ignoring the blaring horns, to where we were standing on the island between the opposing lanes.

Biscuit went into one of his frantic barking fits, but he stopped when she knelt down and let him sniff her hand. "You guys got anything to smoke?" she asked.

Duke looked her up and down and then nodded.

"Word of advice," she said, as my brother began fishing around in his backpack. "This is Jimmy's corner. You boys better fuck off if you know what's good for you."

Duke placed a large flower top of Mexican Red in her hand. We smoked it right there on the street and when we were done, she invited us back to her place.

◾

Samantha lived in a beat-up house next to a Buddhist temple on Keefer Street. She recommended tying Biscuit up in the backyard. The living room had a tan leather couch and a coffee table made out of two milk crates with a mirror resting on top. There were candles stuck in the ends of empty wine bottles all over the floor. The wall behind the couch had holes in it, but it was strung with Christmas lights so it looked kind of cheerful. Aside from the fact that it was a shithole and it smelled real bad, there was something strange about the house. We followed Samantha into the kitchen, where she introduced us to her roommates who were heating up a large can of beans with a propane torch. I don't know who actually owned the place, could have been Jimmy or Lewis or Nigel. I figured it wasn't Samantha because she looked Native and everything that they had ever owned had been taken away from them. I guessed it was inherited—probably Jimmy's because he looked Chinese and this was a Chinese neighbourhood—that, and he talked the loudest.

When Duke rolled a six-paper fatty, they abandoned the beans—and while the six of us stood in the space where you'd expect to find a table and chairs, Jimmy gave us the once-over. "We could use a big guy like you around here," he said, taking the joint from my brother. "Someone to answer the door, intimidate the deadbeats."

"We got a dog," I offered stupidly. "He doesn't bite, but he barks at strangers."

"What is it?" Jimmy asked.

"He's a dachshund," I said.

"A fucking wiener dog?"

I felt a slight twinge of despair as Jimmy collapsed to the kitchen floor, laughing in a cloud of blue smoke. When the joint finally came around, I inhaled long and hard and, as I too slipped into the high, I realized that what was odd about the house was that there was no hum of electricity—no furnace or fridge motor—and in that hollow empty moment of loneliness, Samantha reached into the pocket of her coat and pulled out a delicately folded square of tinfoil and as she opened it, tenderly with the tips of her fingers, it bloomed into a brown rose.

"You guys really want to fly?"

I woke up several hours later in a room that smelled like cat piss; the walls were yellow and the door was charred on the inside from hinge to hinge. There was an old Canadian flag covering the entrance to the closet, which was full of empty Dr. Pepper cans. Samantha tapped on the wall with her long fingernails and stood in the door-way with Biscuit, who was sniffing and scratching at the end of his leash. "Uh, this room's been empty for a while, you guys can stay as long as you chip in for rent."

"Beggars can't be choosers," my brother said.

He got no argument from me; I was busy puking out the window.

∎

The schoolyard across the street had a twelve-foot-high fence that ran the length of the block. At the one end, there was a groomed soccer pitch and a baseball diamond, and at the other, there was a basketball court where we watched a group of kids chump up and down the asphalt in their $200 Nike Jordans—travelling, throwing corkscrews, oblivious to key infractions, bouncing the ball off the rim of the only outdoor hoops we had ever seen with net on them. Basketball was one of the few things we did that truly took us into a comfort zone, a place of concentration, purpose, and satisfaction. When we were hot, nothing could touch us in that sweaty dream. It was our ticket out. Someday, we'd go pro, become stars, buy a house, and live like kings. That night, we tore strips out of the shins of our khakis on the twisted ends lining the top of the fence. Duke had a good four inches on me, so I worked on my floater, the ball hitting the net cleanly. He was a little clumsy and a sore loser though, so I tossed the odd brick or went straight up against him when the score was close. But we always ended our court time with some hot-dogging, Harlem-Globetrotting shit, behind-the-back passes, dime drops, and spins. It took some begging, but eventually I'd get Duke to squat with his hands cupped so that I could actually reach the rim. And hanging there after a backboard-shattering dunk, looking down on my feet high above the court, despite all the shit in the world, I felt like a god. I'd stay up there till my fingers gave out or Duke yanked me down, whichever came first.

∎

Turned out our housemates were slobs, junkies, and thieves. A carton of cigarettes, Duke's favourite Clash T-shirt, and my iPod disappeared in the first few days. Jimmy and Lewis were unapologetic about it; they left their footprints on the mattress Duke and I shared, cigarette butts on the floor. They confiscated anything they thought they could turn into rock or junk. A few weeks later, I got my hands on a car stereo that I hooked up to a battery. We only had the one CD that came with the stereo, a Leonard Cohen disc called *The Future*. The day it disappeared I found Jimmy, Nigel, and Lewis passed out on the living room floor, a cheap red candle, a burnt spoon, and a scrap of tinfoil on the coffee table; the slobs even shared one needle. I swear Jimmy would hawk his mother's ashes if he felt that the urn was worth anything. I found the car battery in the kitchen sink. It's still there.

When Biscuit went missing, I freaked out. My brother said he must have run off, slipped through the hole in the screen door. "Maybe he's sniffing his way back home," he offered.

I tried to imagine a dachshund out there on the Coquihalla, making his way towards the Alberta border.

"Good riddance," Jimmy said when I asked him about Biscuit.

"You're so fucking dumb, you don't even know a good guard dog when you see one."

"Fuck that," Jimmy replied. "He barks at everything; he barks at you for fuck's sake."

Jimmy laughed at me when I shoved him against the fridge. Unlike Duke, I got emotional when I got mad—teary-eyed and angry at the same time. Jimmy was several years older than me, much taller, and he was the kind of guy who might crack you in the head with a cast-iron frying pan if one was handy. Duke had to step in.

"What happened to the dog, Jimmy? We've had him since he was a puppy."

I knew Duke was pissed off too, but he's unpredictable; he could brew for hours, days, and sometimes weeks before he would explode. You never knew when it would happen and it was rarely in the face of what inspired the anger in the first place. The other night, driving low through the key, he dropped me with an elbow to the face. I ended up on my ass, blood dripping onto my shirt. A blink of an eye later and he was helping me up.

"That's for taking my last cigarette this morning."

He was as bad as the old man sometimes.

Jimmy and Duke backed down when Samantha walked in the room. I heard the fork that Jimmy had clenched behind his back fall into the kitchen sink.

"You gotta keep a lid on it," Duke said later. "You gotta appreciate the fact that we have a roof over our heads for dirt cheap."

He was right, and sometimes those shits would even share a score, although it was usually Samantha behind any communal gestures.

By the end of the month, our squeegee gear was gone too.

■

I was sitting on the porch, staring at the lights that ran down the face of the dark mountain across the inlet one night, when Samantha came home. Telling her about my birthday wasn't planned, but it was practically the first thing that came out of my mouth, maybe because Duke completely forgot.

"So how old are you?" she asked, one foot on the step exposing a naked leg from under her faux fur coat.

"Sixteen," I lied.

"So you're not a kid anymore."

I felt pretty certain that I was still a kid, but it sounded nice. It always felt nice when Samantha was around.

"Yeah, I can see it," she said, squinting back at me in the darkness. "You look different."

I offered her a cigarette. She took it, tucked it behind her ear, and then pulled me up from the step and led me over to the alley between our house and the Buddhist temple. The alley was narrow and filled with garbage—blown-out radials, busted lawn chairs, and stacks of unused shingles. After she drew a fresh line of vanilla-flavoured Chapstick across her lips, she said happy birthday and got down on her knees.

I was speechless, up against the splintered siding of the house, my pants around my ankles. I had never done any drug that made me feel better than I did right then. Was this some form of religious bliss?

Did enlightenment have anything to do with a soft, warm mouth, a simple rhythm? I felt acknowledged—a combination of being seen and seeing at the same time. Like I was hanging from the hoop, but now it wasn't asphalt below me, but polished hardwood, a roaring crowd, a sense of belonging, a sense of relief.

I didn't tell Duke, but he knew something was different about me.

"What is up with you these days?"

"I found religion."

"Fuck off."

Time tumbled and staggered in the chaos of that house. There were gaps in my memory. Nobody knew or cared what day it was. Lewis disappeared and no one mentioned him again. Biscuit was gone, the weed was gone. Somewhere between here and there, we had become like the rest of the shit in that empty house—broken, unsalvageable junk—and by December, we owed Jimmy $1,200. He was getting thinner and talking louder and was threatening to boot us out or cut our throats. We needed money, and more than that, we needed drugs.

The next day, Duke convinced an old lady to buy our basketball for twenty-eight dollars. I almost started crying as I watched her hurry down the street with the ball pressed awkwardly against her chest.

"That ball was worth a hundred bucks," I said.

"It needs air and the grip is going on it."

I was shaking my head as Duke recounted the money in his hand. "This ain't going to get us anywhere."

"Beggars can't be choosers," he said. "Unless you got any better ideas, quit complaining."

"We should try breaking into houses," I offered. "Jimmy knows that guy. We can turn over electronics and jewellery fast and easy."

Duke's eyes brightened.

"We'll be smart about it," I said. "We'll only hit the wealthy neighbourhoods."

He threw his arm around my shoulder. "Like Robin Hood."

"And we'll get a new ball—an official NBA game ball."

"Yeah," he said. "We'll do just enough to get flush and then we'll get a place of our own."

■

We focussed mostly on the West End, where the property value and quality of merchandise was much higher, and we were doing okay there for a while. We were making money and we were slowly paying off our debt, but we were cold and wet and shaky from the drugs. By the time February rolled around, our habit had gotten so bad that we were barely breaking even. We were hungry, twitchy, and feeling desperate. I couldn't think of anything I wanted more than a hot shower.

When we headed out into the rain that night, it felt like I was going to freeze to death. My socks were soaked by the time we made it to the end of the block, where I stopped in front of a house with no lights on. I couldn't stop shivering.

"You okay?' Duke said.

I nodded my head, but I was crying too. I hoped that Duke wouldn't notice 'cause of the rain, but I could tell even in the dark that he was looking at me funny.

"C'mon," he said.

We went in through the basement window and found ourselves in a room with a pool table, a big, comfy couch, and a pinball machine. At least in the dark, the stuff looked to be in good condition. Duke said we'd need a U-Haul to move any of that. The main floor was clean and homey, but there wasn't a stereo, TV, or computer to be found. One room was practically empty, except for a few, scattered cushions—nothing but seven white candles in front of a big, marble statue of a guy sitting cross-legged in the corner on the floor. The statue was about two feet tall, a giant flower resting in his cupped hands. Up close, I could see that his eyes were closed, and despite the hairline crack that ran from his left eyebrow to the top of his right ear, he looked content, his mouth revealing nothing—oblivious and aware in the same moment.

When Duke called me from somewhere in the darkness, I lit one of the candles and followed his voice up the stairs to the second floor.

I found him in the bathroom.

"Blow that out," he said.

We undressed down to our boxers in the soft glow of the street-light outside, drew the curtain, and stepped into the shower. The hot water felt like a blessing, the soap smelled strange and woody. My brother's voice humming softly made me smile in the dark. I was reminded of a time when we felt almost normal, the moments in between when we were in a lull. It was like the turning of a page, the three of us at the dinner table, my father contently chewing on a pork chop, Biscuit under the table, waiting for my next secret offering of cooked broccoli. Anything seemed possible in between the raging fits and the drama of my dad's bipolar swings. Since we had left, those peaks of terror had flatlined into a cold desperation and need—constant efforts to keep it all pushed down, the senses dulled by booze and drugs. Under the pulse of that hot shower, we were warm and clean and high, a combination that was rarely experienced at once.

"Next place we live, let's have hot water," I said.

"Yeah, and our own bedrooms."

"And we could get a new dog." I said, optimistically.

"And some fuck'n furniture, no more milk crates for a coffee table" Duke said, softly.

"Maybe we could get a couple of jobs," I offered. "Stop using."

Duke didn't respond and, though my eyes were closed, I felt him move away, his body tensing. And for a moment, it felt like I was standing next to my father. "Sorry," I whispered.

I was rinsing the conditioner out of my hair when we saw the headlights outside the window. Duke tore half the shower curtain down, grabbed his clothes, and struggled to get his wet legs in his pants. I stood there, unsure of what to do. I wanted to stay. Part of me imagined finishing the shower with a cup of tea and a snack. Hell, I'd sit down to an hour of algebra if it meant I could end the night in a real bed. I wanted more of this strange serenity. But Duke had that frantic look in his eye, the one that drove him to move so fast. He was already throwing his shoes and shirt out the window onto the roof of the porch when I turned the water off.

I heard the front door opening downstairs when I heaved myself up onto the window ledge. I wanted to leave a note apologizing for the mess. I wanted to promise to come back and clean it up. I wanted to thank them for the half hour of peace, explain that I had been touched, had realized the possibility and value of a home.

It was still drizzling, cold and steady. Duke was nowhere in sight. And just like that, I felt that same sense of loneliness that I'd felt when we left for the bus station. We had run away, travelled several hundred miles, spent the last six months chasing a high. I remembered my father's words, "You goddamn kids will be back." As the wet cement slowly absorbed the heat from the bottom of my feet, I realized that we had never really left.

My nerves tightened, my mind rushed with adrenaline, my extremities went numb. I pushed it away and tried to hold on to the warmth, to stay with my beating heart. With each step, I pushed against the cold rain. I pushed against the darkness. I pushed against the things trying to make me forget that I still had a chance. I pushed until I couldn't push anymore and, when I opened my eyes, I was on the other side of the fence, standing there in the key, my clothes in a soaking heap at my feet, staring up at the hoop, far, far out of reach.

THE UNCANNY DEMISE
OF JIMMY GARDNER

The mirror Jimmy is staring into only confirms that he has good reason to feel bad about himself. His skin is acne scarred, freckled, pale, and showing the signs of aging that he, now forty-one, is certain will eventually render him an ugly and unlovable old man...a toothpaste stain on his pyjamas suggests the drool and incontinence that are surely also part of this destiny. But it isn't the future, bleak as it is, that is troubling Jimmy so much as the unrelenting regret of the past.

When he was boy, Jimmy Gardner was a shy, good-natured kid who read Isaac Asimov novels. He was a solid B student and, while not athletic, he did watch the Toronto Maple Leafs every Saturday night. But the two most definable aspects of his life were his melancholic disposition and his love for the piano. While he struggled with a persistent sense that the world was going to come to an end at any moment, Jimmy felt blessed with the knowledge that he was good at something, showed promise even. He had, according to his piano teacher, Miss Rosenthal, a natural gift, potential, if he worked hard enough. He practised his arpeggios every day after school; worked on tone, character, and expressiveness; and got good enough that there were times when he managed to completely lose himself in the music. When this happened, Jimmy felt the world and its troubles evaporate. His mind, his heart, and his fingertips were all in accordance with the beauty and brilliance of the composition. It was in these rare moments that he felt truly and fully alive.

Jimmy's tastes were primarily inspired by Victor Borges, Elton John, and of course, Franz Liszt. He imagined a life on the road, performing one night with the symphony, the next to a sell-out crowd in a stadium, and the next in a private concert in Weimar for the Grand Duchess Maria Pavlova. His dream was a multi-genre triptych in which all things were possible. International stardom, virtuoso ability, and time travel. But somewhere along the line, the world began to conspire against him. By the time he was fourteen, Jimmy was overweight and several inches shorter than his classmates. A performance he gave in front of the school that year was met with polite applause in the auditorium, but later in the halls, the jeers and laughter broke his heart. "Classical music," he was told, after being shoved hard against a locker, "is for old men and queers." To Jimmy's knowledge, he was neither of these things, but that was all it took. He went home and told his mother that he never wanted to play piano again.

When Jimmy's mind returns to the present, he reaches for the mirror door and begins sliding it back and forth. His sad face and the items on the shelves within the cabinet appear and disappear. Jimmy's sad face; a bottle of Restoril; a toothbrush; toothpaste; a bottle of Tums; a comb; and a triple-blade, disposable razor; Jimmy's sad face; a bottle of Restoril; a toothbrush; toothpaste; a bottle of Tums; a comb; and a triple-blade, disposable razor…the repetition of which produces the same alluring effect commonly employed in advertising which aims to associate one thing with another. Eventually, the toothbrush, toothpaste, bottle of Tums, comb, and triple-blade, disposable razor disappear altogether. All that remains is Jimmy's sad face and the prescription drugs.

He picks up the container of sleeping pills and shakes it. He hears a satisfying rattle that inspires him to read the label and do some quick math. Dosage, age, weight, toxicity. But once again, according to his calculations, God, or whatever is in charge of such things, had designed the universe in such a way that if Jimmy wanted something, the odds were always in favour of ensuring that he would not get it. The conclusion that there are not enough pills left to do the job inspires him to throw the bottle at the wall. As the handful of pills bounce and scatter, he is aware that even these feeble attempts at catharsis leave him feeling inadequate and pathetic.

According to the self-help books, Jimmy is a poster boy of depression. His father, who Jimmy hasn't seen since he was four, was manic, so he had the genetic thing going against him; he recently found out that his wife had been having an affair for the past two years; and Jimmy had just been fired from his job, which had something to do with his behaviour after he found out that the affair his wife was having was with his boss.

And so it is no wonder that Jimmy is still in his pyjamas at 4pm on a Tuesday, contemplating suicide—converting fractions to decimals, subtracting x, and multiplying y. x equaling his options, y representing the odds of failure. It is imperative, he thinks, that he situates the concept of his demise in a sound, mathematical framework so that whatever method he chooses to end his life will conclude as a final and indisputable fact. The problem is, Jimmy also suffers from a tendency to drift, especially when under stress, into nostalgic ruminations inspired by his favourite TV shows—breakfast at the Cleaver residence, lunch in Mayberry, dinner with Uncle Disney. When things got really hectic, he'd sometimes retreat into an archive of fabricated memories—his mother pulling him along a leaf-laden path in a wooden wagon, his father hoisting him above the heads of a crowd at the zoo, kissing Bianca under an old willow tree at sunset, or the dancing particles of dust in the spotlight as he rises from the piano bench to an applauding audience in a sold-out auditorium in Vienna.

But now, even his fantasies are beginning to show the wear and tear of time. These safe places have grown damp and musty, a little out of focus, and as such, quickly give way to the slightest disturbance.

"I think you're having a mid-life crisis." The words are so vivid and clear that Jimmy scans the mirror, half-expecting to discover someone in the washroom behind him. But all he finds is the memory of a conversation he once had with his wife. He can still see her there in the tub. He had just finished brushing his teeth when she pulled the plug and, as the soapy water began to gurgle down the drain, he paused with his hand on the door, took a deep breath, and told her what had been on his mind for months. "I want to be a father," he said. Fatherhood seemed like the perfect solution to every complaint he could think of. To vicariously revisit specific junctures of childhood, make the right decisions this time. All he wanted was a second chance—to crow and swoon into a graceful arc, arrive at his child's bedroom window, and invite him or her out to play—Jimmy Pan.

And then, as if she had read his thoughts, his wife started to laugh. "You must be joking," she said. "You, a father? You're still a child yourself. I can't believe you sometimes."

Of course, she was right. What was he thinking? Why would his wife ever want to have his child? And my goodness, why would Jimmy ever want to bring a new life into this troubled world, especially with his genetic offerings?

Jimmy watches a single tear form in his eye and then run down his cheek. The fact that he cannot feel the sadness that usually accompanies the shedding of a tear confirms the full extent of his depression. "This is my point exactly," his wife had said when she saw that he was crying. "You need to grow up."

And now, twenty-seven years after he had last rested his fingers on a piano, six days after his wife had left, and eight minutes after deciding once and for all that he had had enough, he raises his head and looks up. While his gaze does penetrate the ceiling and continues on past the interiors of the apartments above him, it does not reach the clouds or the residence of some higher power. Instead, it stops at the gravelly roof of the building itself—its view of the surrounding city and its unobstructed edge. One step into zero.

The elevator makes several stops and, while Jimmy endures a number of strange looks inspired by the fact that he is still in his pyjamas, when he reaches the top floor, he is alone. When he exits the elevator, he finds himself in a narrow hallway. There are no apartment doors and the drywall is pocked with holes. Jimmy walks down the corridor to a graffitied door. As soon as he steps onto the roof, he is rethinking the sketchy equation that had motivated each slothful step to the elevator doors. Given optimal conditions, a man weighing 170 pounds would need about twelve seconds to reach terminal velocity, and given that this was a four-story building, he would likely hit the ground in less than a second, meaning he might reach, if he is lucky, a top speed of about thirty miles per hour before impact. Better try to land on my head, he thinks.

Despite these reservations, he feels a magnetic pull across the gravel to the roof's edge. As he surrenders to this force, he takes in the grey sky, trees and buildings in the distance, the world going about with its indifferent business. When he gets to the edge, he is surprised to find that the gravitational pull he had been feeling has evaporated and that, for the first time in years, he feels a lightness that is so surreal and comforting that he slips into another one of his imaginary drifts—to soar out into the sky, *second star to the right and straight on till morning.*

And for a moment, the desire to jump is replaced with the desire to fly. But his rational mind and its math remind him that no one remains a child forever. All dreams eventually give way to the hard, cold fact that life hurts. The only thing certain is an equation of force, mass, and resistance with a predetermined and unequivocally terminal conclusion. Solid math. Solid concrete.

The fantasy and its reprieve give way like everything else to the unrelenting force of his depression.

When Jimmy takes that final step out into the air, the past, the present, and the future converge. The regret, pain, and the heartbreak all give way to the rush and gut-dropping sensation of gravity. But Jimmy Gardner's life does not flash before his eyes. There are no profound revelations. Instead, he simply falls and, as predicted reaches a speed of thirty miles per hour before his body slams hard into the sidewalk below.

When he opens his eyes, what he sees is a pair of red All Star Converse sneakers. The word "zap" printed in heavy black marker across the white toe of the one on the left, a lightning bolt on the other. He tilts his head slowly and tries to focus—blue, faded denim, patches on the knees, an oversized hockey jersey loosely covering the hips and belt. The hands are small, but the fingers are long and elegant. After his eyes finally make the slow, four-foot journey up to the boy's head, Jimmy recognizes the red ball of hair, the colour of an October squash. A head of hair that attracted humming birds and bumblebees, vigorous scrubbings from complete strangers. Hair that demanded so much attention that people rarely looked him in the eye. Hair that would prematurely recede across his forehead, be cropped short, tuned low to a dull rust by the oxidization of time.

The boy has no idea that he is looking at himself, never would guess that he would be balding at forty, that he would ever wear such funny-looking pyjamas. He is simply on his way to his piano lesson, happy because playing the piano is the only thing that makes him feel confident, but frustrated by his inability to reach the octaves in order to play the cadenza in his favourite piece of music. He can't speak of these things to anyone because these are his private thoughts—things that he is still struggling to understand.

When Jimmy tries to move his fingers, a spike of severe pain somewhere between his ears confirms that he is not only incapable of moving, but that he has indeed failed once again. According to his psychiatrist, all of Jimmy's problems are a manifestation of an emotional sense of inadequacy. "Somewhere along the line, you made a decision to let a preconceived notion of failure determine your life," he had said. "At some point, you will have to revisit that moment and confront whatever deeply rooted trauma set you on this path. In order to reset and take control of your life, you will need to experience a symbolic death."

And now, as Jimmy looks into the boy's frightened face, he feels compelled to tell him not to give up. But when he opens his mouth, a gurgle of thick blood spills out over his chin. The moment the boy starts to cry, Jimmy has the sense that he is in two places at once. He can feel his ribs collapse into his lungs, the air growing thick, each breath becoming laboured, and, at the same time, he feels a sense of purpose that is accompanied by a strange feeling of accomplishment.

As Jimmy closes his eyes, he hopes with all his fucked-up, neurologically impaired conviction that, if and when he wakes, it will be the boy's dream not his.

MOURNING, AFTERNOON, AND NIGHT

Two photographs sit on the night table next to my bed. One is of my father, taken last year while I was visiting him in Toronto. It reminds me of who I am—I can see myself in his smile. It reminds me that I am not alone in the world, that I am loved and safe. The other photo is of my mother. It was taken fifty-four years ago by my father on the day they met. The photo of my mother reminds me of when I was a child, frightened and confused, afraid of the dark. It reminds me that even though we grow up, part of us stays behind. Part of us hangs on to what we have lost.

My mother died when I was nine. She fell down one day. As out of the blue and as simple as that. My dad got Mrs. Patel next door to come over and then he took my mom to the hospital. It was a Sunday. I remember because my dad was watching golf and my mom was getting ready to go to a yoga class at the recreational centre down the street. From where I was sitting on the floor reading the comics, I could hear both my mom humming in the bathroom down the hall and the quiet voice of the commentator on the television. And then I heard the thump of my mother's body hitting the floor.

My dad came home from the hospital alone. He said mom was sick and that it was going to be just the two of us for a while. Said he wasn't sure how long she'd be gone. Said that we'd have to be brave and strong when he came home from the hospital the next day. Said *tomorrow* when I said I wanted to see her. Said *poor little things* when the goldfish bowl got dirty. Said, *oops* when the towels in the bathroom started to smell funny. Said *use Kleenex* when the toilet paper ran out. Said *goddamn* when there wasn't anything in the fridge to eat. Said *I don't know, I don't know.*

One night, instead of a bedtime story, he brought the photo album with the cameo of a white butterfly on the cover into my room and propped a pillow up on the bed beside me. "It's a book of memories," he said. "A world frozen in time." We slowly flipped through the pages and I pointed at faces and he made me guess who they were. I mostly guessed wrong. "That's your aunt Theresa. That's my old friend Oscar. That's your grandparents when they got married."

"Which ones?" I asked him.

"Which ones, what?"

"Which grandparents?"

"The ones in Australia. Your mom's mom and dad."

"The ones I never met."

"That's right. They live on the other side of the world."

"Why is there no colour?"

"Because the whole world was black and white until the day you were born."

I knew that wasn't true. There were plenty of pictures of my mom when she was pregnant and they were in colour, but I was too busy feeling sad to care.

When we came to the picture of my mom catching snowflakes on her tongue, my dad fell silent. She was young and beautiful and the photo, though it was a little bit blurry, made me miss her even more than I already did.

"That was the day we met," my dad said. "She hopped into my cab at the airport and handed me a piece of paper with an address on it. We were on the 401 when the snowstorm started. She was ecstatic, wanted me to pull over then and there on the highway, but I waited until we got to the address on the paper, which was better because the snow by that time was half a foot deep. I had a camera in my glovebox."

"She's so happy," I said.

"Yes," he said. "It was the first time she had ever seen snow."

When my dad quickly flipped the page, his eyes fixed on a photo of a boy sitting on a picnic table, eating a Popsicle.

"That's you," I said.

"That's me. When I was about your age."

"You look sad."

"Yeah," he said. "That picture was taken on the day my dog died. My father had wrapped him in a bath towel and buried him in the backyard."

I had seen the picture before, but he never told me the part about the dog.

"Everything dies," he said.

"Even you and mom?"

"Each and every one of us."

"Even me?"

"Yes, but first you have to grow up and live a long, long happy life."

He hugged me tight with the arm that was already around me and then he looked back at the photo of the boy on the picnic table.

"The sad part," he said, "is that after all these years, I can't remember the dog's name."

It was at that moment that I realized that all the things we were looking at were gone, that photos were pictures of the past—not *frozen* in time as my dad had said, the people and things in the photos were *erased* by time. The dog, the snow, my grandparents. Not only do each and every one of us die, but the memories die too. When my dad turned the page, I was trying not to cry.

"What is it?" he said.

Something had clamped down on my heart and it was making it hard to breathe. "I don't want to look anymore," I said.

My dad closed the album and, even though he stayed with me, I couldn't seem to stop crying. As he held me, he told me not to worry, that there was nothing to be afraid of, and that tomorrow would be a happier day. But when he turned out the light and left my room, I could sense that the terrible thing that had upset me was now lurking under my bed, and while I couldn't actually see the gleaming white teeth, the long pointy snout, or its heaving chest, I could feel its presence, its patience, its hunger. I lay there sobbing in that darkness, thinking about my mother's face, the snow, the black-and-white world of all the things that don't exist anymore.

When I woke up the next morning, I was lying in a damp pool of pee. By the light of day, it all seemed so silly and yet, I couldn't stop myself from telling my dad that there was something under the bed.

When I got out of the bath and went back to my room, my dad had gathered my sheets into a bundle and opened the window to air the room. He said that there is no such thing as a history-swallowing monster. He groaned as he got down on his knees and lifted the skirt draped over the side of the bed. "Just a bit of dust and, oh wait, there's that sock we were looking for the other day." As he held the sock up, he smiled, but his eyes were still sad. "I guess we shouldn't have thrown the other one out."

I looked down at my bare feet. "One sock is no good," I said.

During breakfast, we sat in an uncomfortable silence, looking at the empty space at the table, the washing machine clunking in the closet down the hall.

■

The last time I saw my mother, she was pale and skinny and she had something on her face to help her breathe. She was sick, I knew that, and even though I didn't understand what a brain aneurysm was, I knew in my gut, in my heart, and in the shadowy parts of my mind, that it was serious and bad. I remember wanting her to open her eyes. In some backwards way, it felt like I was the one disappearing and that if she would just look at me and say my name, it would be okay. But all she did was lie there, asleep, even though it was the middle of the afternoon.

Later that day, my dad took me to the park. Said *your mother is dead, it's just you and me now.* Said *we'd have to be brave and strong.* Said *it's okay to cry.* We ate ice cream and watched the ducks. I asked my dad if mom had gone to heaven. He said, *I don't know.* Said, *maybe, yes, that's a nice thought.* I said, *I hope there is snow there.*

We had hotdogs for dinner. Sat on a park bench and licked mustard off our fingers. My dad said mom liked the spicy sausage, would cover it in sauerkraut, eat it with a root beer.

As soon as it got dark, I started shaking again. My dad put his arm around me and asked if I was cold. I said no. We went home and my dad let me stay up late watching television. When I got tired, he carried me to bed. When he turned out the light, he said I didn't have to go to school the next day. I didn't fall asleep. I just lay there in the dark, shivering. I peed my bed again.

When I stepped out into the hall, I could see that my dad's bedroom door was closed, but the light was on. I knocked quietly and then pushed the door open. He had fallen asleep with the photo album on his chest. All the lines on his forehead were gone. He looked a little bit like the black-and-white boy he used to be. The moment I touched his arm, he opened his eyes.

"What is it?" he said.

"I can't sleep."

He placed the photo album on the night table, lifted the covers, and I climbed in.

I felt the warmth of his body and I felt loved and safe, but as soon as he reached for the lamp, I started to cry.

"It's okay," he said. "I'm here with you."

And as we lay there like that breathing in the sadness that had become our lives, I tried to get at the fear that I was feeling.

"Dad?"

"Mhmm."

"What if the same thing happens?"

"What thing?"

"Like your dog. What if we forget her name?"

I felt his hand fall gently on my head. "We won't forget," he said. "We'll say her name every day." His voice was quiet, almost a whisper. "And we'll talk to her and we'll think of her when we eat strawberry ice cream, when we open Christmas presents, when we go for walks in the park, when we make pancakes, when we swim in the lake, when we smell flowers, when we walk in the snow, and when we..." my father's voice trailed off for a moment, "when we go to sleep."

The next morning, instead of school my dad took me to the funeral parlour. We sat in a room in front of a big desk and talked to a man who kept smiling at me.

"You need new shoes," my dad said in the parking lot.

"What's morning?" I asked.

My dad looked at me. "It's when the day begins. When we get up."

I was confused.

"Oh," he said. "You mean 'mourning.'" He looked down at his own feet and frowned. "It's what we're doing now. It's feeling sad."

We had French fries for lunch in the food court at the mall. I got a new pair of shoes. We threw the old ones in the trash. The new shoes were nice, but they felt funny, like they belonged to someone else. When we got home, I had a blister. I tossed one of the shoes under the bed and went to feed my goldfish. One of them was floating on the top of the fish bowl.

"Dad!" I yelled.

He was sipping a coffee in the living room, feet up, watching the news.

"Yes?" he called back.

"Do fish sleep?"

"Yes, they do..."

I tapped the glass of the fish bowl. "Number Two is sleeping."

I heard him fold the paper, groan as he got up, his slow, easy stride across the floor, and then I felt his hands on my shoulders.

And as we looked at the fish resting on the surface of the water, my dad said, "his name was Rufus."

"Whose name was Rufus?"

"My dog," he said. "I just remembered."

The next day, Number One died, too.

We buried the two fish on the same day we buried my mother. We stopped in the park on our way to the cemetery and, as my dad stood there holding the spoon he used to dig the fish grave, he asked me if I wanted to say anything. I stood there, looking down at the little pile of dirt, the popsicle-stick cross I made. "One and Two," I said. "They were good fish. They liked to swim and watch me eat breakfast. They came to say hello when I fed them. They couldn't live without each other."

And that's how I learned to call things by their names, give voice to what had previously been too difficult to utter. My mother's name was Rachel. She liked spicy sausage and root beer, wore rings on every finger. She had blue eyes, brown hair that turned blonde in the sun. She came here from Australia. I have a photo of her when she saw her first snow. She died when I was a little boy.

My dad's name is Thomas. He has grown old. He limps when he walks. I call him now once a week and tell him how things are. He still likes golf and reads the newspaper. I visit on holidays, Thanksgiving, Christmas, and on the anniversary of my mom's death, I always spend the night.

I've grown up, stopped being afraid of the dark, stopped wetting the bed, but I still say her name before I go to sleep and my father still sleeps with the light on.

FAMOUS WOMEN I HAVE LOVED

When I was boy, I had an undiagnosed visual impairment that made the world a blurry, vague, and treacherous place. The fog around the edge of everything I looked at turned things like stairs, bicycle rides, and sports into precarious challenges that usually ended in injury. I had to sit in the front row in the classroom so that I could decipher instructions on the chalkboard and, in an effort to avoid being picked on in the schoolyard, I spent my lunch breaks in the library, where I could sit quietly and escape from all the things that frightened and alienated me. All I had to do was grab a book, lean in close, and my imagination did the rest.

My favourite book was filled with paintings by the Group of Seven, distorted landscapes that seemed to perfectly reflect a world that I longed to live in. I spent countless lunch breaks paddling a dark Algonquin lake in the back of Tom Thomson's canoe. Flip a page and I'd be wandering through broadly painted forests, studying clouds that drifted above windswept conifers. For me, those surreal paintings were like a sanctuary, a place where I could wander and drift without the worry of injury.

When I was diagnosed with what ophthalmologists call *low visual acuity*, the glasses I had to wear did nothing to alleviate the bullying I was hiding from, but that was a small price to pay for the world that opened up to me—things that had once appeared as vague shadows and smudges now bloomed before my eyes. Geometric and organic shapes revealed their textures and edges, distances became negotiable, words and sentences were no longer indecipherable codes. When I opened a book, I could see the stark whiteness of the page giving shape to each letter and word. I began to devour whole paragraphs in seconds, chapters by the hour, novels by the week. As I fell in love with Juliet, drifted down the Mississippi with Huck and Jim, sailed the seas with Ishmael, my imagination began to expand beyond the limitations of my insecurities. I became a willing heart ready to embark on whatever journey the author had in store. And then, in the first semester of grade 10, just as the bell rang to signal the end of lunch break, I closed the book I was reading, looked up, and there was Sasha.

I don't know how long she had been sitting across from me, but at that moment, the sun cast her in a golden meadow of light and I couldn't seem to take my eyes off the knit of her sweater, her slender neck, the line of her nose curving into her brow. From where I was sitting, she looked like something that fit perfectly into the red maples, windswept pines, and rocky lakes of my imagination. When she noticed I was staring, I took off my glasses and pretended I was cleaning them. She closed the book she was writing in, and though the detail was gone, she was close enough that I could see that she was staring back at me. "You live on Beech Street, right? In the house with the gravel driveway?"

I nodded.

"I live across the road. Number forty-two."

"Hi," I said.

She started gathering up her books. "Better hurry," she said.

When she got up to go, I was holding my glasses up to the florescent lights as if I was checking for smudges.

"Aren't you coming?" she asked. "History class, it starts in five minutes."

I made a concerted effort to gather the objects in front of me into a pile, but I eventually had no choice but to put my glasses back on, and when I did, I was shocked to see that she was still standing there.

"I like your glasses," she said. "They make you look like a scientist, or like something nocturnal, an owl, maybe."

A minute later, we were walking down the hall to history class together, as if it were the most natural thing in the world.

"I want to try them on," she said.

Before I could answer, she handed me the books she was carrying and removed my glasses. I slowed my step and, despite the sudden blur, tried to act as if everything was fine.

"It's like a dream," she said. "It's all distorted and surreal."

And for a moment, we were both impaired, unable to negotiate distance and detail. But then she was off. She began to leap and spin. I did my best to keep up with her, and while I couldn't quite hear the music that surely inspired the cadence and rhythm of her dance, the hall turned into a Group of Seven painting, as distorted and surreal as the pounding in my heart.

She stopped *en pointe* in front of the classroom door. "I'm going to be a soloist," she said, handing me my glasses. "Run my own dance company."

After I gave her back her books, I applauded her performance. She took a bow and then headed into class. I waited a moment before I put my glasses back on because I wasn't ready for the dream to end.

I went to the library after school that day and headed straight to the Performing Arts section. I read every book I could find on dance. The theories, the technique, the history. With its origins rooted in ritual—to appease a nature spirit—I discovered that our dreams were not incompatible at all. I became Sasha's fan.

◾

When Sasha turned sixteen that year, I showed up at her door with two tickets to the National Ballet. While I knew that she philosophically rejected the strict movement of the form—"corsets and points hindered the full expression of the soul"—she once referred to *Giselle* as the *Hamlet* of all dance.

She screamed when she saw the tickets.

"Happy Birthday," I said.

When she reached out to receive my offering, I playfully tucked the tickets behind my back. She stepped out onto the porch and reached behind me, but I turned and raised my hand over my head and then backed down the stairs. I ran across the lawn and she followed. I hopped and spun awkwardly along the sidewalk and she followed. It was childish and crude, but for the minute or two that it lasted, it felt like Sasha and I were dancing together. I leapt from the curb—and she followed.

I didn't see the pickup truck hit her, but I heard the screeching tires behind me. When I turned around, she was suddenly and impossibly far away, several metres up the road. When I got to her side, the sharp focus of it was unbearable. There was gravel imbedded in her chin, her hair had bits of dirt and dust in it, one of her shoes was gone, and her leg was twisted in an awkward and grotesque position. The music in my head went silent.

In the waiting room at the hospital with the rest of her family, the nurse informed us that Sasha's leg was broken; more specifically, she now had a steel rod from knee to ankle, supporting her shattered tibia. There was also some undisclosed damage to her pelvis. "She'll be okay," the nurse said. "But she will have a permanent limp."

Sasha was sent home in a cast with a wheelchair and a prescription. For the first week, she stayed in bed with the curtains drawn, refused to use the wheelchair, and only got up to go to the washroom. While she welcomed my visits with a pained smile, seeing her lying there day after day in the dark watching the spare television that her mom had set up on her dresser broke my heart.

I wanted to apologize, to let her know that I wished it was me that had been struck by the car, but all I could manage to do was stand there at the foot of her bed and gaze at her despondently.

"Look," she finally said, "the only thing worse than people feeling sorry for me, is people feeling sorry for themselves."

She turned her attention to the television. A very long moment passed without either of us speaking. The volume had been turned down and so the soap opera that was on seemed extra stupid and meaningless. I took off my glasses to soften the sharp edge of the guilt I was feeling. "Will you be able to dance again?" I asked.

She aimed the remote at the television and when the screen went black, the room fell into darkness. I heard her wince as she shifted her weight on the bed. "Everything hurts," she finally said. "But it hurts most when I cry."

I couldn't say what made her snap out of her funk, but the next time I visited Sasha, the television was off and the curtains were open. "I'm glad you're here," she said, shifting her weight to the edge of the bed. "The doctor says I need a hobby, something to keep me stimulated as I recover." It seemed to take all of her strength to haul herself up. For a moment, I thought she was going to collapse, but she managed to stay on her feet. "He says I need to be patient and that eventually I'll have to reevaluate my objectives, maybe even reinvent myself." When she got to the closet, she pulled the door open and stood there for a moment, scanning the shelf above the hangers. "There it is," she said, pointing at a box. "The big one marked 'Art Supplies.'"

A half hour later, she was perched on the edge of her bed, her extended leg resting on a chair as she squeezed a coil of vermillion red out of a tube. "The light in this room isn't the greatest," she said, "but I'll make do."

She took to painting as if she was born with a brush in her hand. She began with still lifes, filling canvas after canvas with images of meticulously positioned fruit and vegetables. There was a seriousness to her work. Each stroke of the brush was as fluid as any gesture she had ever articulated as a dancer, but her gaze, which had once contained an outward expression of bliss, transformed into a concentrated look of agony.

While dancing had been performance based, painting was a private affair. Sasha had rules for anyone fortunate enough to be permitted into her creative space: never open or close the curtains without consultation, always ask permission before looking at a work in progress, and do not absently pluck an apple from a bowl, especially if it is bruised, because you may be messing with something symbolic and personal.

By Christmas, the cast was off and she had turned her eye to the mirror. Her frustration and pain was evident in every piece and the discarded canvases protruding from under her bed were piling up. Her work had become dark and disturbing—fragmented facial features put together in monstrous ways, an exorcism in progress.

"They're self-portraits," she said.

When I asked her to paint me, she declined.

"It would break your heart to see yourself through my eyes," she told me.

I took down the picture of Isadora Duncan that hung over my bed and replaced it with a portrait of Frida Kahlo.

In my final year of high school, a series of headaches led to a battery of eye tests. The specialist seemed worried. "I think you were misdiagnosed," he said. "There's evidence of cell disruption in the central portion of the retina. We call this *vitelliform macular dystrophy*. It's going to get worse." I stared at the smudged features of the doctor's face. "Aspirin will help with the headaches," he added, "but there's no cure."

The next day, I was sitting on the floor with my back against Sasha's bedroom door, watching her work. She had been silently staring at a freshly gessoed canvas for several minutes. There were dry smudges of paint on her forehead, I could see that, and she was biting her nails, something she did when she was uncertain about how to proceed. It was enough to bring a tear to my eye.

"Let's run away," I said to her.

Her face tightened in concentration and, as the seconds passed, it seemed like she wasn't going to answer.

"Where on earth would we go?" she finally said, still staring at the canvas.

I wiped at my cheeks with the palms of my hands. "We can hitchhike north, live in the woods."

When she turned to look at me, I saw that she was now crying too. "In case you haven't noticed," she said, "I don't paint landscapes."

I had never heard her use that tone of voice before, nor had I seen her move with such brute force when she shoved the canvas and the easel to the floor.

"I don't know who I am anymore," she yelled.

My heart clenched as Sasha stormed about the room, crushing tubes of paint, snapping brushes, and tearing the pages out of a Diego Rivera book I bought her.

I got up, opened the door, and stepped out into the hall so that I didn't get in the way or otherwise interfere with her latest performance.

The transition from painting to photography was as sudden and violent as her departure from dancing. There was a growing intensity in her focus and concentration, as if she was trying to fit herself into something that could not contain her. Taking photos of neighbourhood cats, flying birds, children running—seemed to be her way of slowing the world around her down. It was as if she wanted to hold everything still, so that it could feel the same constraints that burdened her. As the months went by, her work got more and more technical and precise. Tripods and close-up filters were employed. And while my eyesight continued to worsen, I could see just how awkward and painful it was for her to get around. Once she was positioned and ready to shoot something, it took a great deal of concentration to get back up from the lawn or steps on which she had positioned herself. I helped her as much as I could—not only did I learn about lenses, f-stops, aperture, and shutter speed, but I also familiarized myself with the work of the photographers that inspired her—Dorothea Lange, Jessie Tarbox Beals, and Imogen Cunningham. And as Sasha hobbled about from one photographic study to the next, I remained her audience, her fan, her adoring admirer. I didn't say anything about the dark circles under her eyes or that her work had become forensic; instead of capturing the essence of movement, her photos seemed to contradict the nature of it. Nor did I mention that she had become addicted to the painkillers that she said she still needed to stave off the constant ache in her hip.

She always seemed to be dealing with a degree of pain, but it seemed to worsen at the end of the day. The pills in her pocket rattled when she walked and when she emerged from a long session in the makeshift darkroom she constructed in the basement, she always looked pale and vaguely perturbed. I rarely saw her eat and when she did, she'd follow whatever she had consumed with a pill. The eight-by-tens she began producing were mostly over-exposed images of her bare feet.

I was not all that surprised when she gave up photography, but I was relieved to note that it did not involve the destruction of what I knew to be a very expensive camera. The carnage this time was more psychological. She began to stay up late, sleep in, and the poetry she began to write was fragmented and coded, just like her kaleidoscopic search for identity. While she experimented with line breaks, meter, and alliteration, she drew further inward. Moving slowly, limping from one poem to another, Sasha began to channel her pain and sorrow in brooding metaphor, imagery, and connotation. As usual, I did my best to keep up with her. I ordered large print copies of the poets she mentioned, tried to give her constructive feedback on the work she produced, and as Sasha wrote odes to the vanilla-scented heliotrope, the Lady's Slipper orchid, and a knot of blue field violets, I fell in love with Emily Dickinson.

I began to wonder if Sasha would ever find the artistic vocation that would satisfy her, and I began to wonder if she would ever love me the way I loved her. "It's complicated," she said one evening. We were sharing a stolen cigarette in her room. "I love you, but I can't love you."

That was the moment when I realized that I couldn't really see her anymore—that she had become a blurry, undefinable thing. The only thing that was clear was that I would be lost without her. I smiled and said, "I love you, but I can't love you—that sounds like the name of a poem."

After dropping the cigarette butt into an empty wine bottle, she made her way over to the stereo and put on a record. The soft swirling snare, the steady walk of the bass, and the smoky lilt of the piano cast Sasha in a transformative light. When she began to sing along, her sultry and sullen voice was perfectly suited to the melancholic timbre of the music.

"What's this?" I asked when the song ended.

"It's called 'Lady Sings the Blues,'" she said.

She slipped into her new obsession as if it were a long, red dress. She cut her hair, started drinking whisky, and when she landed a Sunday night spot in a piano bar, she dropped out of university and bloomed in the spotlight. With mascara running down her cheeks and an awkward tilt in her hips, she rambled through the standards like a soul-broken diva. "I Don't Want to Cry Anymore," "Good Morning Heartache," "When Your Love Has Gone." And in the blur of those coloured lights, time flew by, my eyesight worsened, and I was introduced to the fullest manifestation of her personality I had seen. Before either of us knew it, Sasha acquired a manager, a record deal, and an invitation to take her show on the road.

■

I was living in a small bachelor suite in the basement of a triplex when she showed up drunk at my door with a suitcase in her hand. I hadn't seen her in six months. She had sent me a letter or two, but I couldn't read them.

"I need a place to stay," she said.

I opened a bottle of wine, massaged her feet, and listened to her recount the joys and tribulations of life on the road. She drifted into a half-conscious rant about being born fifty years too late, how people don't appreciate jazz like they used to. When she eventually fell asleep on the couch next to me, I tried to imagine the details of her face, the years of frustration and pain evaporating, a trace of the child and the surreal wildness that drew me to her all those years ago.

In the morning, as I got ready for work, I made an effort to avoid banging into the shadows. I left a note telling her to help herself to food and laundry if she needed it. I called to check up on her several times throughout the day, but there was no answer. When I came home, it was apparent by the bathrobe she was wearing and the smell of coffee that she had just gotten up. She was grumpy and distant. She ate dinner without saying much more than thank you and then she started drinking again. She left the apartment that night around nine and came home well after I had gone to bed.

We entered a new and more intimate chapter in our relationship, but I knew enough about Billie Holiday to doubt it would last. While her wounded animal routine worked very nicely on the stage, her volatile moods were hard to negotiate at home. She was living out her latest persona to the fullest—the whimsical, free spirit dancer was gone; the reclusive painter had been exorcised; the photographer that never fully developed had given way to the poet. When she locked herself in the bathroom with a bottle of gin, I wondered just how much of the hard-luck jazz singer I could take. What began as a fitful rage eventually tapered off into an incomprehensible muddle and ended with the sound of an empty gin bottle hitting the floor. I closed my eyes and waited because, though I wasn't certain exactly what she was metaphorically going through, I knew she was changing yet again.

When she finally emerged from the bathroom, I barely recognized her. "Okay," she said. "Let's run away together."

And as I made my way to the bedroom, she followed. And as I imagined that we were changing together, the two of us slowly making our way towards an incarnation in which there was room for both of us, she followed. And as I thought of the time she put on my glasses and danced down the hall while I slowed my step and reached for the wall, she followed. I took off my clothes and climbed into bed and she followed. And when I turned off the light, I saw that she was, just like the distorted and surreal images in the Group of Seven book, a blurry childhood dream that I would never see again.

AFTERWARDS

According to some folks, purgatory is an interim state in which the souls of those who die are made ready for heaven or hell. Some folks would have you believe that piety, which is to say, prayer, giving alms, and fasting can influence where those in this state end up. They believe purgatory is a place where sinners and saints alike have the chance to balance life's accounts, settle debts, make amends, and otherwise redeem themselves. Some pilgrims will even tell you that purgatory has a geographical bearing on earth—a cave on an island in Ireland or a mountain situated diametrically opposite Jerusalem.

I'm here to tell you that while it is true that purgatory is a place where those that decide such things determine who goes where, just how that decision is made has little to do with the prayers of the living. The fact is, your final destination in the ever-after is determined by a game of strategy, tactics, threats, and sacrifices. In short, a different ball of yarn altogether.

You may be asking yourself what makes me such an authority on the subject and, such as it is, I make no claims to be wiser than any other soul. And while I ain't never studied theology or otherwise had any formal training, when it comes to speaking on the matter at hand, I do so with a degree of confidence because I happen to be the fella whose responsibility it is to repair and maintain the border between damnation and salvation. While that may sound like a lofty and somewhat far-fetched claim, truth be told, the divide I'm referring to is little more than a splintered wooden fence that runs along a grass meridian between two lanes of traffic—one goes one way, all paved and smooth, while the other runs in the opposite direction, gravelly and full of potholes. As rustic and rudimentary as this fence may be, it has kept all manner of souls from going astray for a couple of eternities. And as eternities are hard on all things, every now and then a nail comes loose, a rail needs to be replaced, a post needs shoring up, or someone like the fella I'm about to tell you about comes along, and well...

■

I had just tied up my mule and was leaning over the lowest of three rails nailing a fresh length of cedar to a vertical post when the stranger arrived. I'd been watching him coming for quite a spell—the dust his car had been kicking up on the rutted gravel he was driving on could be seen for miles. He parked next to the remains of a derelict Volkswagen and, as he climbed out of his car, a whisky bottle dropped from his hand and smashed on the gravel. He stood there cussing for a minute, and then after delivering a halfhearted kick at the glass and dirt, he turned his attention to the boarded-up shop fronts, the dusty curtains drawn shut at the hockshop, the overturned garbage bin in front of the drugstore. Eventually, his eyes came to rest on the two fellas playing chess by the gate about fifty yards further along. One sitting on one side of the fence and one sitting on the other, the chessboard, as it were, perched on the rail between them.

The stranger stood there, as I had seen so many newcomers do, with a perplexed look on his face. You can almost smell the wood burning as they try to figure out where exactly they are. But soon enough, the racket I was making with the hammer drew his attention in my direction. As he crossed the street, I admired the fine cut of his expensive-looking suit—an interesting contrast to the run-down backdrop of the shops behind him. He had a hesitancy in his step, but his eyes were friendly and the car he drove, which was mid-size and North American-built, was still in operational order. In short, one would be hard-pressed to be sure which side of the fence he belonged on. At that point, the game had pretty much just started and so he was, I suppose, for the time being exactly where he ought to be. As he got closer, I noticed the tattoos on the backsides of his hands. On the right was the homemade, faded, greenish sort you see on sailors, criminals, and all other manner of reprobates. 999, it said, but of course I knew better. On his left hand, he sported a colourful and intricate cross—fine lines and shading—clearly the work of a professional. But the one feature that made it clear who had the upper hand in the match down the way was that there upon his shoulders rested a small contingency of bees.

"Howdy, mister," he said.

I peered up from my work and smiled.

"What's with the fence?" he asked.

I shrugged my shoulders all innocent-like.

"I don't believe I have ever seen an old wooden fence running through the middle of a town before."

"It's a historical thing," I offered. "Municipal heritage and all that." I could see that he wasn't buying it. "You must be new in town," I threw in, changing the subject.

He squinted at the blooming cherry trees and the brightly coloured shops with their window boxes of flowers behind me and then turned to glance back at the dilapidated stores on his side of the fence. "Is there anywhere I can get a Scotch in these parts?"

"Whisky?" I echoed. "I reckon The Ossifrage Tavern," nodding to the right. "About a half block down the way you came."

I turned my attention back to the hammer in my hand.

"What about over there, on the pretty side?" he asked, raising his eyebrows toward the manicured boulevard behind me.

"No alcohol over here," I said. "Dry as prohibition. No whisky, no beer, not even wine."

He was still standing there when I finished driving in the nail.

"I'm a working man, myself," he said. "I sell bibles. The good word of the Lord—leather-bound, softcover, pocket-size, CD-ROM, and, wonder of wonders, I even have a couple in Braille."

"Don't bother with literature myself," I said. "Never had much cause."

"What about the wife, children, friends? Everybody knows someone who could use a little soul healing."

I eased my back up straight. "Just me and old Molly," I answered, nodding towards my free-range mule, who at that moment was standing on the sidewalk behind me in front of the post office nibbling on a planter full of nasturtiums. "And to my knowledge, she never learned to read."

I bent forward and set another nail. With each swing of the hammer, the stranger flinched as if each blow was driving the spike into his body. He was still standing there when I finished with that nail too.

"I don't suppose I can persuade you to join me for a drink, can I? The first one is on me."

"No can do," I told him. "I hesitate to state the obvious, but I'm on this side of the fence. And well, you and the Ossifrage are on that side."

"Well, just slide between the rails there. The Ossifrage, as you say, is just down the road."

"I'm obliged," I lied, "but I gotta get back to work."

He looked both ways up and down the street. "Well, come now," he said. "A quick drink won't do any harm. I'm sure this old fence will still be here."

"I don't mean to be rude," I told him, "it's just that rules is rules."

Something in him hardened then. It was subtle, but his muscles tensed and a deep line formed on his brow. I wondered if I might have to call security because the bees, who had until that point been as content as if they were resting on a summer rose, began to hum and buzz. I could see that he was aware of this too because a single bead of sweat rolled down his forehead. He inhaled and closed his eyes. A long minute passed, during which he just stood there still as a statue holding his breath. And in that calm, the agitated bees seemed to settle down as well. When he opened his eyes again, he had a look of relief on his face. And as he slowly took a breath, smooth and easy like, he reached inside his jacket and withdrew a business card.

"In case you change your mind," he said, holding the card up in his fingers.

Jesus Saves was emblazoned in metallic blue in the centre, and below it was the name *Judas*, followed by an email address.

"Unfortunate name you got there, mister," I said flatly.

"Actually works in my favour," he said. "People seem to respond to the irony."

While the sun on the side of the fence I was on had cast the grass under my feet in a lovely diffusion of light, the jaundiced, halogen quality of light on his side of the fence was beginning to heat up. Several more beads of sweat formed on his brow. He loosened his tie and then slowly undid the buttons on his blazer. As he did so, the bees rose in unison, lazily circled his head, and then settled once again on his shoulders.

"What's with the critters?" I said.

"*Apis mellifera*," he whispered, as if he didn't want them to hear. "Otherwise known as the honeybee. It's the darnedest thing, but they have been following me for—" he paused and glanced at his wrist as if to consult a watch, "well, since I can remember."

"Bees. Beelzebub," I muttered under my breath.

When the church bell at the corner behind me sounded, Judas's attention was drawn back to my side of the fence.

"I don't know if I was hit on the head or what," he said, rubbing his neck, "but I can't seem to remember how it is that I got here. In fact, I don't even know where exactly here is."

I knew that it was just a matter of time before all the mystery was gone from it, but some folks are simply too thick in the head and have to come to it slow and hard. "Maybe you need another good knock on the head to set things right," I offered.

"Well, the only thing for certain," he said, fishing a hanky out of the back pocket of his trousers, "is that it sure is getting hot out."

Just as he started dabbing his forehead, the doors of the church opened and a small crowd stepped out onto the street, some settling for a chat in the dappled light under an alder tree. A smile came across Judas's face as his long, crooked shadow stretched through the fence, across the boulevard behind me, and fell upon the red shoes of a little girl balancing on the curb.

"Well, good evening," Judas called out from his side of the fence.

A cold breeze arose out of nowhere and I could see the hem of that little girl's dress ruffle around her knees and her arms pucker with goosebumps. At that moment, her mother broke from the crowd, rushed over, and steered the girl back towards the church.

"You'd think she just saw the devil," Judas said.

I glanced over at the two fellas up the road who were still deeply immersed in the game. "It's just that fraternizing over the fence is frowned upon," I said, hoping not to confuse things too much.

"Well, you and I have been having a nice chat and no harm has come of that."

"As the custodian of this fence," I said, "I am obliged on occasion to consort with folks on both sides, but I was hired as much for my carpentry skills as for my ability to remain impartial or otherwise nonpartisan."

"Nonpartisan, as in non-religious?"

"Non-biased, non-affiliated, non—just about anything you care to name."

"Sweet Lord Jesus," he sighed. "God is my witness, I am not a preaching man, but I am deeply concerned whenever I find myself in the company of a non-believer."

"Lots of souls that need saving at the Ossifrage," I said.

The notion of a whisky, which is to say, the possibility of mixing business and pleasure was all it took to distract him. Judas licked his lips and glanced back down the road. "You sure you won't join me?"

"Fence ain't gonna mend itself," I said.

And with that he strolled off in his slow and easy way back to his car.

"I should mention," I added, catching him in the middle of the road, "I don't know if they allow bees in the Ossifrage. What's more, I don't think they allow bibles in there either."

Judas made an adjustment to his tie and straightened his posture. "That is the problem with you agnostics," he said. "You aren't up with current realities. Nietzsche was wrong—despite the separation of church and state this past century, we are at the height of our spiritual enlightenment. The good Lord is alive and well, but so is the devil, and thank the bells of Trinity for that, otherwise I'd be out of work. If you want to do the work of the Lord, you have to go where the devil lives."

He turned again and started walking as if he were balancing gracefully on an invisible line. "And mark my words," he said over his shoulder, "the bees, nuisance though they may be, are as much a part of God's will as the bible and the whisky."

When he got to his car, he took off the wedding ring he was wearing and tossed it into the back seat. He looked back at me for a moment, smiled, and then climbed in behind the wheel. He backed out and drove in reverse the half block down to the Ossifrage, where he parked in front of a rusted sign that read "Handicap Parking Only." Judas then unloaded a pile of bibles from his trunk and carried them into the tavern.

I never did mention that most newcomers leave that fine establishment either at a full sprint or dragged out by the ankles.

■

After making certain that the new rail I had installed was good and secure, I placed my tools in the box, gave my old mule a good scratch, and then grabbed myself a piece of grass in the shade. Don't know how long I slept, but when I awoke, the sun was setting and the low light had cast a beautiful hue on the flowers blooming on this side of the fence, while a hollowing wind was rattling the bare branches of the trees on the other.

I had just gotten to my feet when I noticed that Judas was standing under the bare bulb on the Ossifrage's veranda, whistling as he counted a large stack of bills. How he managed to convert those bibles into cash in there was beyond me. He flicked the cigarette he was smoking onto the ground, took a long, deep swig from a bottle that he had tucked up under his arm, and then glanced over my way. When he saw me, he raised his hand full of bills, waved, and stepped down to the street. Though I couldn't be sure from that distance, he seemed to be quite pleased with himself. I chuckled as I watched him try to unlock the door of the wrong car—same colour, but you had to be as smashed as a sailor to mistake the two. The bees must have been a little irritated by his lack of grace as well because as he climbed into his car, he was cursing and swatting in the air around his head. He slammed the door hard, turned the ignition, and then pulled out into the path of an ill-fated wind.

I don't know where exactly Judas thought he was going in such a hurry, but when the dust settled, there were bibles all over the gravel road, pages ruffling gently in the now-faint breeze. The car, which had a large hole in the windshield, was accordioned around a Dead End sign and Judas was lying in a bed of petunias on this side of the fence.

When I rolled him over, I saw the gaping wound on the side of his head and the shards of glass and blood in his eyes. The bees settled back down on his shoulders as if there was nothing more natural than congregating on a man whose face was all busted up. After a moment, Judas stirred. He struggled to prop himself up on his elbows, blood trickling out of the gash in his head as slow and thick as honey. Though his bloodied eyes were swelling shut, I knew he was watching me as I tied one end of the rope to my mule and then moseyed on over and set about tying the other end to Judas's ankles. When I got that done, he made a sound that left a red stain of blood all over the front of his shirt. It was hard to make out, but I'm pretty sure he said something in the neighbourhood of: "The damn bees stung me."

"Rook to c2," I said.

I set my mule in line to drag Judas back to the other side of the fence; glancing over at the two gentleman playing chess down the way, I saw one adjust his crooked halo, the other contemplatively swing his bifurcated tail as he put his opponent's king in check.

"Giddyup, mule," I said.

It had been decided, by strategy, tactics, or otherwise, and now there weren't nothin' Judas or anybody else could do to change it. The game, at least where Judas was concerned, was now over.

THE ART OF DYING

My father was a romantic—not in the Hallmark sense of the word—in fact, my mother always said he was hopeless when it came to Valentine's Day and anniversaries. He was a romantic in that he had a degree in Victorian Aestheticism and could rhyme off long stanzas of Oscar Wilde, Swinburne, and Pater. He loved poetry, always had a book in his hand, and couldn't seem to resist a window with good natural light. He wasn't interested in small talk or what was going on in the news and he tended to drift out of conversations at the dinner table, but if you would listen, he'd tell you everything there is to know about how he believed poetry to be the conciliator of nature and man.

When I was thirteen, he spent some time in the psych ward at the hospital. I remember my mom crying as she poured herself a drink. "Your father has a melancholic nature," she said. "He gets into these funks and sometimes it takes him a while to feel happy again." I didn't know what that meant exactly, but my mom was having a hard time catching her breath so I nodded and kept my mouth shut. The next day, I pulled a dictionary from the shelves in my dad's office. Melancholy: *noun, plural melancholies* 1) a gloomy state of mind, especially when habitual or prolonged; depression. 2) *archaic.* a condition of having too much black bile, considered in ancient and medieval medicine to cause gloominess and despair.

When my father came home from the hospital, he looked tired and old. He slept a lot, hung around the house in his bathrobe, spoke even less, and didn't seem very interested in eating. He was what my mother called mopey. One day, he sat down beside me at the kitchen table and for a moment, he just sat there looking like he was trying to make his mind up about something. I was about to get up and leave the table when he told me that a poem had once saved his life. "Emily Dickinson," he said. He played around with the serviette holder for a moment and then asked me if I wanted to hear it. I did. I closed my eyes as he recited the poem by heart. I don't think I really understood it, nor do I remember what it was called, but it had something to do with a bird, a worm, and a beetle.

What I do remember was the rhythm in his voice—the look of sadness on his unshaven face, the long silence that followed. I remember him getting up and how it took him a second or two to straighten his back. "I'm going to take a bath," he said. I remember how he stepped forward and gave me an awkward hug. I remember him whispering into my ear, "Find a girl and love her with all your might." I remember noticing, as he left the kitchen, the quality of the light coming in the window and how it illuminated the spot where he had been sitting. I remember thinking of Alexandra, the girl that I had a secret crush on. *Love her with all your might*—is that what I was doing? I remember watching television, losing track of time, the smell of grilled cheese sandwiches when my mother asked me to tell my father lunch was ready. I remember knocking on the bathroom door and getting no answer. I remember opening the door and the feeling of the water soaking into my socks, the white-and-black ceramic tiles around the sink, the yellow cup with the three toothbrushes in it. I remember the reflection in the mirror of my father lying in the tub, his skin parchment white, the water blood red. I remember drawing the shower curtain, stepping back out into the hall, and closing the door.

The whole thing seemed so surreal. Part of me stayed there in the tub with him or part of him followed me out of the bathroom, I'm not sure which, but I would never be able to separate myself from the cold, hard will of the despair that drove him to end his life. I wandered back to the kitchen in a daze, unable to feel anything but a sense of dread and gloom. My mom knew what had happened as soon as she saw me.

On the day of the funeral, I locked myself in the bathroom, ran the water, and stepped into the tub. As I lay there in the cold water, I knew that I had a melancholic nature as well. It was there in my eyes, in my heart, in my DNA. I let the full, tragic weight of it pull me down. They would find my body days later, I thought, fish eaten and bloated. Friends would gather in consolation. Alexandra would keep my obituary photo under her pillow and cry herself to sleep every night. I was thirteen and I was doomed by the fates of genetics, tragedy, and poetry, which would shape the narrative of every relationship I would ever have.

By the time I was in high school, I had no illusions about my position on the fringe of the cliques that made up the school's social order. My marks were decent, especially in English, history, and geography, but I couldn't seem to integrate with my peers. Their conversations about sports, television, and music didn't interest me. I liked reading books about tragedy, romance, and unrequited love, but no one I knew gave a shit about poetry and literature. Keeping a low profile seemed like the best way to avoid the awkwardness. I spent my time moping about, morbidly pondering the ways that I could put an end to the loneliness and alienation that followed me from one class to another. And then I fell in love with Janice.

She sat in front of me in English, and while I had lost myself in the sheen and sun-touched quality of her hair on several occasions, I was pretty certain that she didn't know that I existed until the day she turned to ask me if she could borrow a pen. In the brief moment that our eyes met, the clouds parted and a ray of light came in through the window and illuminated her face. The space around her was glowing, radiant with confidence and electricity. When she reached for the pen I had dug out of my pencil case, our fingers touched. I don't know if she noticed it or not, but there was a spark. I felt it travel through my fingertips and run up the length of my arm. It was there pinging through my veins as we took turns reading stanzas from Irving Layton's "Whatever Else Poetry Is Freedom." And it was there as I followed her to her locker after class and then all the way to the chess club where she and twelve other kids met every day after school. When I walked in the room, she handed me a sign-up form and paired me with a kid with thick glasses who spoke broken English. It didn't take long to figure out that the ability to think several moves ahead, while at the same time being prepared for the strategies of my opponent was simply beyond me.

When Janice and I finally faced off, a wooden board and thirty-two little chess pieces the only thing between us, she took my king in six moves. And that was it. Janice shook my hand. It was cold, devoid of anything other than sportsmanship. "You may be better suited for something less strategic," she said. "I hear the badminton club is looking for people." Her indifference was heartbreaking. I retreated to the nearest boys' room where I locked myself in a stall. And that was when it happened. I was struck, as if by a silver bullet of clarity. And with the barrel of the imaginary gun I had pointed at my forehead still smoking, I wrote Janice a poem. I only remember that every second line rhymed and that it would probably be best categorized as an ode. And even though Janice would never read it—it was written on the stall door in the boys' washroom—it was my first attempt to convert the loneliness and despair I was feeling into poetry.

I spent the next three years scribbling in a journal, filling its pages with my heart's longings, angsty thoughts, and epiphanies. Much of what I wrote at that time was inspired by Verlaine, Rimbaud, and Baudelaire, voices that seemed to articulate the symbolic, the tragic, the allegorical, and the sensual. I had come to believe that poetry was the key that would turn the heart of the girl whom I would eventually *find and love with all my might*. These last words of my father and the sense of duty they imparted were acutely in tune with my romantic longings when I first laid my eyes on Judy. I had just pulled a copy of Verlaine's *Romances sans paroles* from the shelf in the school's library when I heard the sound of a book hitting the floor in the next aisle over. Peering through the space between the shelves, I saw her bend and then straighten up holding a hardcover exposé on Martina Navratilova. Judy was wearing, like the photo of the tennis player on the cover of the book, an outfit that revealed a long, slender body, the sight of which lured me out of my deep, dark funk. I smiled awkwardly at her through the gap in the shelves. "Hi," I said. To my surprise, she smiled back and returned my greeting.

I saw her again the next day, but before I could get her attention, she disappeared into the gymnasium. I pulled the door open and stood next to the fire exit watching with newfound fascination the girls' senior volleyball team gather for practice. I was sixteen, my hormones were raging, and the poem I wrote attempted to juxtapose the intoxicating quality of skin and muscle with the music-less pitch of the coach's whistle, which spiked painfully through my brain every time a drill ended.

This particular infatuation was different in that Judy, the Olympian goddess, stimulated a number of erogenous zones I wasn't even aware existed. At the end of the practice, I hurried down the hall, taped the poem to her locker, and waited by the drinking fountain. I was close enough to see her blush. And then, instead of crumpling the poem up into a tiny ball as so many other girls had done, she took the gum out of her mouth and used it to secure the poem to the inside of the locker door. That simple gesture was enough to inspire me to approach her and introduce myself. She smiled again, told me her name, and when we parted, her phone number was written in ballpoint ink on the back of my hand.

I took up residence in the bleachers, both in the school gym and at the courts where she took private tennis lessons three times a week. I carried her gym bag and listened to her worries and her aspirations—her top spin and floating slicer needed work, but her game close to the net was strong. When she came home from a weekend-long tournament to find me standing forlornly on her drive-way, she waited until her parents were inside and then backed me up against the garage door and kissed me. All the stirrings in my body converged into a single current that left me in a state of adrena-line-induced euphoria. I thought that this was it. Thanks to poetry, I was finally having my first real relationship. I was ecstatic, but with it came an awakening to the will and torment of lust. Being close to Judy made my body shake. It was magnetic and intoxicating, but with each clumsy advance towards her breasts, it became clear that her athletic agility was not limited to varsity competition.

"I can't visualize it," she said. "I need to be able to see it before it happens."

Judy's reflexes and my inability to integrate myself into the realm of her concentration, speed, and timing-centred goals certified that I would never become her lover.

When she received an out-of-province athletic scholarship, I was devastated. We spent an hour on her front porch making promises that we both knew would never come to pass and then she kissed me tenderly and said goodbye.

As soon as I got home, I swallowed half a bottle of Aspirin and spent the evening cramped up on the couch pathetically drying my tears with a sock stolen from her gym bag. As I drifted off into sleep, the thought of dying a virgin propelled me to the bathroom where I shoved my fingers down my throat and tried to regurgitate every suicidal thought I had inherited.

■

It had been two years since my last date when I met Suzanne. We met in a line up in the university cafeteria during a break in a lec-ture on twentieth-century Russian literature. She had her hands full with her cellphone, a bag of chips, a chocolate bar, and a large coffee. When her phone began to ring, I offered to help. As we walked back to class together, she ate and talked and I learned that we were both

Nabokov fans. Though I regarded *Pale Fire* as his greatest achievement, she preferred *Laughter in the Dark*. Over dinner that night, I discovered that she was on antidepressants, that she had her own apartment, she smoked a lot of marijuana, and she was a feminist, but only when it suited her.

During the six months that Suzanne and I were together I adopted her lifestyle—staying up late, sleeping in, and spending too much of my time smoking pot and playing board games. Once, in the middle of a game of Scrabble, after I managed to spell the word *moribund*, she said apropos of nothing, "As long as you're willing to help me with my essays, I won't give you a hard time about your dour sense of humour or the disturbing nature of your poetry." These spontaneous and candid confessions always caught me off guard, but my anxieties were quickly softened by a hefty toke from a homemade bong. A minute later, we were both laughing hysterically because neither of us could remember whose turn it was. We binged on junk food and ate handfuls of mints in a futile effort to cover the smell of pot. We were high the first time we made love. And though it was over embarrassingly quick, I fell asleep in her arms feeling as if somewhere in that hazy fog there was a glimmer of light and hope.

Suzanne was a composite of all the women I had loved. She was smart, passionate, and fit. But she was, in the end, a bit too much like me.

I had just finished doctoring her draft of a paper on Bulgakov's *The Master and Margarita* when Suzanne's mother died—a late-night collision with a bus while driving under the influence. As Suzanne swooned into a cocooned silence, I felt the cloud of her own melancholic nature. She stopped going to class. She smoked more pot. And she took solace in television and silence. When the phone rang one day, Suzanne just reached for the lighter and the pipe on the coffee table.

"You're not going to answer it?" I asked.

As she inhaled, her face was cast in an eerie orange glow.

"Nope."

"What if it was me calling?"

"How could it be you calling?" she said. "You're here. You're always here."

I remember how she nearly choked on those words as she exhaled a thick cloud of skunky smoke over her shoulder. When her coughing fit ended, she tapped the bowl of the pipe into the ashtray and told me it was over.

Later that night, I locked myself in my mother's Nissan with a hose connected to the exhaust at one end and squeezed into a crack in the car's window at the other. I sat in the driver's seat with a bottle of whisky and a copy of "A Season In Hell" and was about to turn the ignition when I smelled the little, pine-scented tree hanging from the rearview. I thought of Suzanne, her cool, minty breath and her indifference. I thought of Judy, her athletic dedication and her indifference, Janice and her...indifference. Why was I always the one with the broken heart? I vowed then and there to never be the victim again. The next time I felt that familiar sense that I was about to be hurt, I'd write a poem and walk away. According to M. Rimbaud, love doesn't exist.

I went to my room and said goodbye in my journal. No drama, just the simple turning of a page.

I began to wonder if I would ever manage to escape the sense of imminent doom that permeated all the relationships I had ever had. The cloud of depression and uncertainty that followed me around became a constant meteorological condition. I wrote, I read, I drank coffee, and I spent long spells adrift in thoughts that were by design functions of my inability to confront my feelings. And yet, I couldn't seem to shake my father's advice to find a girl. It had become intrinsic to the idea that I would not have lived with any real purpose until I had loved to the fullest of my ability.

I had been spending a fair amount of time at the art gallery where after a stroll through the latest modern art exhibition, I'd take a seat in the cafe to write and soak up the natural light courtesy of the huge window facade. I was in the process of discarding my belief that all poetry is an attempt to repair the fractured state of the heart by giving voice to the things we otherwise cannot speak of. I was trashing this notion in favour of the absurdist's concept that we are compelled to seek value and meaning in a world and yet are unable to find it. I wasn't aware that anyone else was at the table I was sitting at until I heard the unmistakable sound of someone loudly sipping at the contents of their mug. I peered over the copy of Camus' *The Myth of Sisyphus* to find Marianne's unflinching gaze.

"Define a masterpiece," she said.

I considered packing up my stuff and finding somewhere else to read, but I had only taken one sip of my coffee and she was beautiful, a little intimidating, but confidence was something I had always admired. I closed the book and adjusted my beret. "A masterpiece, I think, is ineffable, otherwise it would be diminished by the mediocrity of words."

A long discussion ensued. She was well read and opinionated, more of a dadaist than a surrealist. When the conversation concluded, she looked at me as if I were her next meal. "I live around the corner," she said, "and I make a much better coffee than this place."

I lost the top three buttons on my shirt as soon as we stepped into the elevator.

"It's been a while." She breathed these words into my ear as she placed my hands on her breasts.

Later, as I followed the trail of clothes back to the door, she told me that she had been married twice and divorced once. When I returned to the bedroom with my shirt, belt, and pants, she was leaning against the headboard smoking a cigarette. I had never really felt comfortable naked and here she was making it look so natural and easy. I took a seat on the edge of the bed and while I dressed, she proceeded to describe her exes as if they had failed some fundamentally simple test. "These two men were less than useless," she said. "Sure, they were both good looking, but they lacked the ability to handle and respect an assertive woman."

I appreciated just how casual and uncomplicated it all seemed, and before I knew it, I was telling her that I was genetically predisposed to be another disappointment, that I was the son of a romantic who was afflicted with a melancholic disposition. "I like sensitive men," she said and then she extinguished her cigarette and pulled me back into bed.

She had a voracious appetite. I had never dated anyone who was so willing and shameless. She'd momentarily hike up her skirt in the back of taxis to reveal that she wasn't wearing underwear. She'd flash me in elevators, on woodsy strolls, in the parking lots of bookstores and jazz clubs. When we did have quiet evenings at home, we rarely made it to dessert.

As it turned out, Marianne wasn't obsessed with sex as I had thought. She simply wanted a baby. Three months to the day of our first date, she told me that she believed in me and that despite the genetic pools that we were spawned in, we write our own destinies. And then she told me she was pregnant. "I know it sounds pathetically romantic," she said, "but I fell in love with you the moment I saw you. It was like I had been waiting for you my whole life."

Without a moment's hesitation, I got a job selling shoes at the mall and moved into her apartment. A month later, the second bedroom was furnished with an heirloom crib, a chest of drawers full of little yellow jumpers and socks that fit my thumb. She hummed as she brushed her long, blonde hair, packed me a delicious and nutritious lunch each morning, and despite being overwhelmed by the cyclonic pace of all this, when I caught her unaware sitting in a beam of sunlight, I thought I would never breathe again.

The idea of being a father was humbling, terrifying, and all at once exciting. I was, at least in Marianne's eyes, worthy of such an incredible honour. To be the father of her child meant that I finally had the chance to fulfill *my* father's wish, to love with all my heart.

We took after-dinner walks, laughed about her cravings, argued about potential names, went to prenatal classes, and vowed to never part. I did my best to keep my depressive tendencies at bay and pushed back against the subtle pressure in my chest that sometimes left my heart feeling like an imploding planet. And while my fears and worries never lost their bite, we drifted into a storybook existence of self-medicated domesticity.

And then, in the third trimester, as I made my way down the hall to the bathroom to let Marianne know lunch was ready, I felt a sense of apprehension. In hindsight, I can say I knew something was wrong before I heard her crying. The feeling was always there, no matter how bright the sun or how smoothly the day had been going. I stumbled back to a memory that, despite my efforts to allay it with fortitude and distraction, had never left the orbit of my troubled mind.

I remember hesitating and then opening the bathroom door. I remember the feeling of wetness soaking into my socks. I remember the shower curtain, half of which had been torn away from the rod. I remember Marianne awkwardly reclined in the tub, something strawberry-scented lathered into her hair, and there, between her legs, a cloud of deep, red blood blooming in the water. I remember wanting to turn around, to close the door and walk away, but then something in me snapped. In the grand cacophony of the universe, it was barely audible, but it brought me to my knees, the height of a thirteen-year-old boy looking forward and backward through time. My father's lifeless body, the blood from his wrists indistinguishable from the cloudy vermillion discharge now smudging the water before me.

As I helped Marianne out of the tub, I found myself thinking of that Emily Dickinson poem—something about a bird that bites a worm in two, swallows it raw, steps aside to let a beetle pass, and then flies away. My father knew it by heart and it had once saved his life. But the brutality, the kindness, and the indifference—whatever it was that made so much sense to my father could not make sense of this. In the end, poetry had failed, but this time I would not turn away. I had found the girl and I would hold on with all my might. I would be what my father wanted, not what my father was. I would find a way to survive this, even if it killed me.

OLD HABITS DIE HARD

They had first met at the 7-Eleven. It was 2 a.m. and she was standing out front under the neon light in her red smock taking a smoke break when she saw him step out of a service door from the east wing of the hospital across the road. He was a silhouette at that point, but the aluminum crutches he used to compensate for what she could tell was a sore leg flashed intermittently in the dark. She watched him hobble along the dimly lit path past the benches, the recycling bins, and the ugly steel structure that was somebody's idea of public art. When he stopped at the curb, she was amused by the fact that he bothered to look both ways. There was no traffic at that time of night aside from the distant whine of a siren and the idling taxi at the hospital entrance. As he made his way across the street, she found herself thinking that the red bandana he was wearing combined with the limp made him look like a fucked-up pirate. When it became clear that he was on his way to the store, she stubbed out her cigarette and headed back in to the till, where she could see him between the Coke and Pepsi signs taped to the store window, a sliver of view that framed his progress towards the door. As soon as he stepped into the store's horrible wash of light, she knew he was dying.

"Do I know you?" he asked, as she rang his things through. "You've been staring at me since I came in."

"No, it's not that," she said.

He looked her directly in the eye. "What is it then?"

She didn't look away, but she didn't say anything either.

He rubbed a thumb across his brow. "You lose them in chemo," he said as he tucked the newspaper and the Caramilk bar into his backpack.

She watched him swing the crutches under his arms and turn away.
"What kind of cancer do you have?" she asked.

The question stopped him at the door. He looked around the store. It was empty except for an old guy messing around with the Slurpee machine.

"I'm sorry," she said. "I'm just curious, I mean, I'm studying to be a journalist."

"It's not cancer," he said. "It's karma."

When he showed up at the 7-Eleven a few nights later, she held the door open for him. He shuffled past her without a thank you.

"Don't you sleep?" she asked.

"I'm nocturnal," he said. "Old habits die hard."

He looked a little worse this time, jaundiced in the florescent light. Old and yellow, she thought, and yet there was still something hopeful and determined in his eye.

"Speaking of which," he continued, "I need a corkscrew."

Even though she knew they were out, she found herself pointing to the far aisle. "We might have something next to the light bulbs and stuff." It was a game she sometimes played with customers, a way to break up the boredom, test their patience, see what kind of a person they were. She watched him through the round mirror in the back corner of the store, waiting patiently for him to give up looking. But he was determined, the kind of person who didn't like to ask for help. A few more minutes passed. I should have timed him, she thought. This is a record for sure.

By the time he shuffled back to the counter and placed a Caramilk bar on the lottery display between them, she had made up her mind.

"Chocolate to go with your wine?" she asked.

"This crap is made from cocoa beans grown by slaves who can't afford the product they make."

The remark and the anger in his voice seemed to come out of nowhere.

"Then why are you buying it?"

"It's for the security guard who lets me back in."

She glanced out the window, across the dark street, and over at the lights of the hospital.

"I was planning on a little vino, but it's not my night, you are out of corkscrews."

"Hang on a second," she said, reaching into her front pocket. "You can borrow mine."

He took the Swiss Army knife and placed it in his jacket pocket. "You're a lifesaver," he said.

She pointed at her name tag and smiled.

"Nelly," he said. "Nice to meet you; my name's Libra."

■

The latest treatment hadn't been going so well. The rash covering his chest and the swelling of his feet had everyone perplexed. The oncologist had had a look the night before, taken some notes, and then left him with an uneasy smile. Libra slept fitfully. When the doctor came by in the morning, she told him that he had been scheduled for more surgery.

He was contemplating a jump from the hospital window when he heard someone tapping on the frame of the door.

"Enter," he said, leaning forward to see who it was.

He almost didn't recognize her. Her hair was up and without the red smock, she looked older, like a young woman instead of a girl. She stopped at the foot of the bed and tossed a newspaper in his lap.

"Are you lost?" he asked.

"You haven't returned my corkscrew."

He leaned over to the bedside table and picked up her army knife. "Sorry," he said, "they've been giving me some kind of sedative to help me sleep."

An awkward moment passed, in which he found himself smiling at her for no reason.

"Here's the deal," she said, "I have an assignment due in a couple weeks and I need someone to interview—it's a course requirement." She reached into her purse and revealed the top of a bottle. "I bring you what you want and you let me ask a few questions."

He was beaming like an idiot now. "It all depends," he said, "on whether it's red or white."

She took a quick look towards the door and then pulled back the paper bag to reveal the label. It was red, which was good, but it was Canadian.

He insisted that they do this on neutral ground, away from convenience store lighting and hospital apparatus. "There's a place to sit by the window at the end of the hall," he said. "It's quiet and there's a lovely view of the concrete and asphalt below."

He made it on his feet as far as the elevator doors, but despite his efforts to appear able and virile, he eventually surrendered to the wheelchair she offered.

"Think of me as your chauffeur," she said, as he settled back into the chair.

After she parked him by the window, he watched her use the corkscrew on the bottle.

"You look a little like Hugh Hefner," she said, as she discretely filled two paper cups with wine. "Sad and yet somehow mischievous in your bathrobe and pyjamas."

The cult of youth, he thought. They act as if they are immortal. She had just compared him to a man twice his own age, but in doing so, he noted, she didn't demean him. He took a sip of wine, hoping for ripe fruit flavours of plum and blackberry, but his palate was numb. The wine was coarse and bitter in his mouth. It tasted like medicine. He raised his cup. "Welcome to my mansion."

A moment later, she had her laptop open. "Okay, she said, "first question."

"Fire away."

"What kind of cancer—"

"Geez," he interrupted. "There you go again. No easing in? No foreplay?"

"I'm sorry," she said.

Her face flushed ever so slightly.

"It's fine, I just don't wanna feel like I'm being interrogated."

"Okay, new question—why do they call you Libra?"

He doffed back the cup of wine and grimaced. "It's a long story," he said. "So I'll give you the Coles Notes version." He held out his cup and waited until she refilled it. "I was supposed to be born in October. My parents had actually planned it that way. They wanted a Libran child—the best sign in the zodiac, my mother thought—John Lennon, Gandhi, and all that. But as fate would have it, I was three months premature."

"That would make your birthday in—"

"July," he said.

"What sign is that?"

His mind immediately went to the scar on his leg, the bitter metallic taste in the back of his mouth, the catheter in his chest. "Osteosarcoma."

"I'm sorry," she said.

"Don't be. I was just answering two questions at the same time."

She was a slow typer and this bothered him. Like her poor selection of wine, it made it hard for him to take her seriously. He was already beginning to regret agreeing to be interviewed. The cancer (or was it the treatment?) had reduced him to a man who needed to rest in between paragraphs of conversation and he had the sense that he was being viewed as an inconvenient but necessary hurdle in the requirements of her journalism degree. He had spent his life pushing back against the injustices of the world, fighting corporate evils, and now he was powerless, reduced to the protocols of the pharmaceutical industry. After the invasive surgery and the bombardment of chemicals his body had been subjected to, the only thing left was his anger and this overwhelming sense of loneliness. The attention of this stranger, as fickle as it may be, was better than nothing, he decided, and so they were both getting something out of this.

"Next question," he said.

When she looked up from the screen, she cleared her throat and sat up a little straighter. "I'm reading this book," she said, "by Jean-Paul Sartre and I was struck by this thing he wrote—something about how we are always heading somewhere; we are never fixed, static, or complete—"

For a moment, it looked like she might start crying. He wasn't sure if he could handle that. He took a sip of wine. "That's not a question," he said.

"I'm sorry. I'm just—"

"Look, everything you will ever need to know about philosophy you can learn from A. A. Milne and Dr. Seuss."

She laughed and that gave him a little bit of pleasure—to know that from this broken, doomed vehicle he could still inspire joy. "In all seriousness," he continued, "Socrates was my hero, but I was a Poli-Sci major." He was about to ask her if she had read Hobbes, Machiavelli, or Naomi Klein when a wisp of blue smoke escaped from his mouth, drifted upwards, and dissipated against the ceiling tiles. He hadn't had a cigarette in ten years. Phantom smoke, he thought. "Did you see that?" he asked.

She looked up from her laptop, her hands still working on the keyboard. "What?" she asked.

He wondered what contaminants still lingered down there in his lungs—in his body's memory. He nodded at the pack of cigarettes lying in the clutter of her open purse. "I still get cravings," he said. "In fact, it has crossed my mind more than once to take up the habit again. It's perverse, but I really don't have anything more to lose." He wondered if he should have been more indulgent in his life, more of a hedonist, less righteous. "I gave up coffee, refined sugars, television, and red meat. And though I still fantasize about a barbecued porterhouse steak on occasion, I even stopped wearing leather products. And now here I am, reaping the rewards of my healthy, socially conscious lifestyle choices."

The indifferent look on her face as she continued to type left him feeling suddenly and deeply hollow. She was young and naive, but she was not innocent. She was part of what he had come to see as the hopelessness of the future, which left him unsure of whether he wanted to slap her or warn her. He opted for the sage. "But seriously, if you are in some kind of an existential crisis," he said, "I'm afraid you've come to the wrong place for answers."

She wrote this down, too, and as he listened to her fingers pecking away at the keyboard, he realized that they were both in a state of crisis—she was looking forward and he was looking backwards, but they were both still looking for answers.

When he awoke that night, it was dark. The air around him felt thick and slow like water. There was a pressure centralized in his groin, otherwise he felt numb and devastatingly weak. He swung his hips off the bed, his knees bent, the weight of his feet on the floor. He scratched his head and glanced over to see if the bathroom was occupied. When his eyes adjusted, he hoisted his weight off the edge of the bed and collapsed into the fog of an anesthetic hangover. When he hit the floor, a bolt of pain thundered through his thigh. He reached for the flimsy section of material just below his left knee and he remembered: they had taken his leg. He had signed off on it, but he forgot to say goodbye. He hoisted himself up and, after balancing on his one foot for a second, he fell back onto the bed. He pictured a garbage bin filled with body parts. He had been reduced. There was less of him now. Less to give. Less to lose. He wept as warm pee flooded his crotch.

She arrived twenty minutes late for their second interview. As each minute passed, he was surprised to find that he was more and more worried that she wouldn't show, but as soon as she did arrive, he felt irritated by her tardiness. He watched her drag a chair across the room and sit down facing him. She didn't apologize, nor did she say a word about his leg, the missing one or the one he had left.

He felt like calling the whole thing off, but when he saw that she was out of breath, he softened. "Are you okay?" he asked.

She nodded. "I'm fine. I had a rough morning." She made some adjustments to the skirt she was wearing and then opened her laptop. "Okay," she said. "Tell me more about yourself. Before the cancer."

He was still groggy and in a state of post-amputation shock, but her presence added a degree of giddiness to his bewilderment. "There's not much to tell," he said. "I spent most of my life trying to save things—old-growth forests, whales, the ozone." He paused for a moment, as if to bask in a time of simpler grievances. "But then things got more complicated. They always do. The G8 summits, NAFTA, the WTO."

"I've heard of those things," she replied. "Quebec City, Kananaskis, Toronto. I watched it on TV."

He imagined her flipping back and forth between the news and the latest reality television scenario until her stomach grumbled and she headed off to meet her friends at McDonald's. For a moment, he hated her, and he could hear the distant cranking of a chainsaw, the rattle of the toggle spinning back into its casing, the revving of ferocious power at the whim of one puny finger. He thought about her stupid blonde streaks, her Nike slave-made running shoes. He was judging her, placing her in a safe place where she couldn't touch him. And as he wondered if the cancer had entered his brain, he was overwhelmed with tears and they came out in a stuttering sob, snot across his lips.

"What is it?" she asked. "Should I call a nurse?"

He wiped at his face with his sleeve and took a deep breath. "What do you want from me?" he said. But as soon as these words left his mouth, he vomited a colourless pool of bile onto his lap. When their eyes met, he covered his face with one hand and pulled back on the wheel of the chair with the other, spinning himself away from her, away from the real question—what did he want with her?

"I'm sorry," he said. "I don't know where that came from." He listened for the sound of her fingers documenting the confession, that hesitant search and tap on the keyboard, but what he heard instead was the sound of her retreat, the rushed gathering of things, an apology, and then the cacophonous roar of being alone.

■

Three days passed before she called. He felt a mixture of relief and embarrassment. He tried to remember giving her his phone number, but he couldn't recall a lot of things lately.

"How are you today?" she asked.

He noted the hesitancy in her voice.

"I'm fine," he lied. "Just got back from a jog around the block."

"Can I come by this afternoon?"

"I've been thinking," he said. "Maybe we should do the rest of the interview over the phone."

"Sure," she said, quicker than he would have liked.

In the silence that followed, he could hear her take a drag on a cigarette. She inhaled deeply and he considered the smoke's journey down her trachea. He had read somewhere that you only exhale about one-sixth of the air in your lungs. The body is a mystery, a traitor. He considered hanging up, but even over the phone he couldn't seem to make up his mind about her.

"You still there?"

"Yes."

"Okay, question. Ready?"

"No."

She took a deep breath. "Is it curable?"

When he responded, his voice was quiet and measured. "They gave me what they considered to be decent odds at first, but things haven't been going so well."

Another long silence.

When she exhaled, he imagined that he could smell the cigarette smoke.

"I'm thinking about giving up journalism and becoming a doctor," she said. "I figure if these so-called experts can't help you, then I'll have to find a cure myself."

"Yeah, well, you better hurry; there might not be much left of me by the time you figure it out."

Her breath was there again. Air, oxygen, vaguely erotic, natural, from her mouth, intimate in his ear. He heard her light another cigarette.

"I get the feeling," she said, "that there is something you're not telling me."

"You sound just like my ex-wife," he said, but he wasn't sure if he meant it or if he was flirting with her.

"You were married?" she asked.

"Off the record, yes."

"What was her name?"

"Never mind about that."

There was another pause. He imagined her looking down at her left leg, lifting it in the air and balancing for a moment on one foot.

"I have a confession," she said.

His throat was desert dry. He reached for the cup of ice on the bedside table and took a few pieces into his mouth.

Her voice shifted a register higher. "I'm not really studying journalism."

He waited for her to laugh, but she didn't.

"I'm sorry," she said. "My life sucks and I thought, I don't know—"

He heard her take another drag on the cigarette.

"I've got problems. I know that. And I don't know what I'm doing with my life, but I need to start over. Can we do that?" Her voice was low and soft again.

He could relate to this despair. It was there inside of him, mixed up with the fear. "Okay," he said. "Let's start over. I have a confession to make as well. I don't really have cancer."

She laughed and he was glad.

"What else do you want to know?"

"I don't know how to say it."

"Go ahead," he said. "Clock's ticking." And it was true, during the moment it took for her to gather her courage, he could hear the tick-tock of every precious second in his heart.

"What I want to know," she said, "is what it's like to be dying."

There it was. He thought about hanging up the phone. But something was different now—no longer bound by an academic or otherwise formal agreement, they were just two people having a conversation.

"Well," he said, "that's a question I'd prefer to answer in person. Do you play chess?"

"Is that an invitation?"

"Yes, I guess it is."

■

He moved a rook across the board and, while she was contemplating her move, he told her, "My testicles are swollen, my fucking invisible leg hurts like hell, and I coughed up about a pint of blood this morning."

"That's not fair," she said.

"I thought you wanted to know what dying was like.

"I do."

Well, I'm sorry to interrupt your concentration, but—"

"This is not sportsmanlike."

He smiled as she committed to her queen.

"On the bright side," he said, moving another rook. "Hair's growing in." He lifted the edge of his bandana to reveal a tuft of fuzz above his ear.

She laughed and made another careless move.

He took her queen. "No mercy."

"You're a scoundrel," she said, as she reached into her purse and applied a fresh coat of lip gloss.

Her lightheartedness made him wonder for a moment if she let him win. "Really, it's all been a series of good days and bad days, but I suspect that someday soon, one of those bad days will sink its teeth in and the game will be over."

"Does it really feel like a game to you? Aren't you afraid?"

He cleared his throat, but then caught himself. He didn't want to lecture her. He was done with that. "I spent most of my life angrily trying to change people's minds," he said. "But now I'm trying to lighten up and not take everything so damn seriously."

When she got up and moved over to the window, he noticed that she was wearing sandals instead of the baby-blue cross trainers.

"Who the hell am I to decide what is right for another person?"

"Do you have many regrets?" she asked.

He closed his eyes. He knew that the answer he was about to give her was the most truthful thing he had said so far. "Yes," he answered. "More than I can count."

■

She had the sense that she was standing on a bridge between where she was and where she was going. Below the bridge was a river. Life was rushing by in a forceful current. The hospital across the road had become personal, no longer an anonymous institution. She had become familiar with its smells and sounds. She had left her fingerprints on the elevator's buttons. She knew the names of three nurses and had eaten the wrapped sandwiches from the machine on the second floor. When she looked back at the store she was surprised to see that her boss was still standing there by the door with her red smock in his hand. She had no idea what she was going to do with the rest of her life, but she knew that quitting that job had something to do with whatever would come next. She turned back to the hospital and just started walking.

■

He didn't say a word until she parked his wheelchair in front of the elevator and pressed the button.

"Whoa, what are you doing?"

"We are going to get a little breath of fresh air," she said. "Relax, I cleared it with the nurse."

In the elevator, he tilted his head back and looked up at her. He knew her presence had nothing to do with anything rational or real. In fact, he was beginning to suspect that she was a hallucination, a morphine-induced angel. "I haven't been outside for weeks."

"Don't worry," she said. "Not much has changed, the world is still a mess."

She rolled him down the hall past the cafeteria, the waiting room, the gift shop, and out the electronic doors. It was raining lightly.

"Hold on," she said, tilting the chair up the curb.

He smiled as they accelerated across the lawn to the shelter of a willow tree.

"There," she said. "We made it."

The rain began to intensify. Cars splashed puddles up onto the sidewalk, random drops falling from the branches above seemed to explode on the exposed skin of their arms.

"Can you feel that?" she asked.

He didn't answer, but he did feel it. He felt a small amount of joy in the discomfort of being out in the chilly, damp air. He stuck out his tongue and caught a drop as it curled over his lip.

She crouched down beside him. "I've got one last question, but you have to promise to answer seriously. No funny stuff."

"Okay," he said.

"If you could have anything right now, what would it be?" she asked.

"Ah, the last wish of a dying man."

"The end of the interview."

He closed his eyes, counted to three, and cleared his head. The first thing that came to mind was the malfunction of his cells. He pictured a battle, a black mass spreading within. He thought about the tasteless hospital food, his bed sores. He thought about the blank space that used to be his future, the long and bittersweet trail of his past, the loneliness that seemed to inhabit each. He thought about a tasteless joke he couldn't seem to forget. He thought about the oceans, the forests, tuition fees, sport franchises—things that no longer seemed relevant in any way. He thought about his ex-wife's breasts, the gentle swell above the v of her favourite shirt. He thought about going back to Greece, the exhilaration of swimming naked, the simple pleasure of washing his hair in the shower. He thought about dancing, foot massages. He thought about the fact that he had always wanted to learn to play the cello. He thought about his failed relationships, the people he had hurt, his susceptibility to hemorrhoids, his degree, his anger and hopelessness for the future, the resulting vasectomy. Somewhere along the line, his words and actions became extensions of his body. He thought about the last strawberry he had eaten. He thought about this strange girl's kindness, her full lips, her slender fingers on the armrest of the wheelchair. He thought about the rain and then he imagined a mountaintop high above the clouds, a quiet calm obscuring the world below. He thought about getting up and walking away.

"More than anything," he said, looking her in the eye. "I would love a cigarette."

∎

She closed her eyes and opened them and she realized where she was. She had reached the other side of something. They both had. She wiped at her cheeks and opened her purse and, after taking out the pack, she placed two cigarettes in her mouth. When she struck a match, it flared and glowed within the harbour of her cupped hands. She inhaled deeply, removed the two cigarettes from her lips scissored between her fingers, tilted her chin upward, and exhaled. She then passed one to Libra.

"Are you sure sure?" she asked.

He took the cigarette in his hand, placed his elbow on the arm-rest of the wheelchair, and brought the cigarette up to his lips. He inhaled gently and closed his eyes. "Interview's over," he said. "No more questions."

And they smiled, knowing that it was the last cigarette that they would ever smoke.

OPHELIA

The set dressing in the theatre of this nuthouse is deceitfully pleasant: four peach-coloured walls, a black vinyl chair next to a bed fitted with baby-blue sheets, a south-facing window with a view of the lake, and, wonder of modern conveniences, an en-suite loo. According to the script, it is a state-of-the-art care facility with twenty-four-hour nursing staff, housekeeping, entertainment, therapeutic fitness programs and a decently stocked library. But look a little closer and you will see the Velcro restraining straps, the barred window, and the embarrassing trail of of urine that leads from my bed to where I am presently sitting on a toilet at God-knows-what hour of the night, praying for a miracle. I close my eyes and push, but my insides feel like knotted yarn.

Not only is my plumbing in ill repair, my aching knees make it difficult to traverse the length of my quarters in a timely fashion and my mind, well, it has become *unreliable*, prone as I am to spells of distraction and meaningless chatter. The doctors here claim that I have a vivid imagination—a common enough affliction amongst those who spent their life on the stage—but they believe I exist in a script of my own making. A tragedy, if one had to categorize it. Lost in time, they say. But of course, they have it all wrong. *Tis in my memory the truth is locked, and I alone shall keep the key of it.* And so, I bare the humilities they subject me to. Canasta, bingo, and sing-a-longs are bad enough, but the daily mopping and changing of the linen and the vile scent of sour decay that no amount of lavender talc will dilute are more than I can bear. Which is to say nothing of the saltwater rinses to quell the bitterness expelled from the back of my throat—exhale, rattle, inhale, wheeze. I refuse to be bathed, you see. I have what I consider a very just aversion to any body of water deeper than my sense of fate. But never mind all that, the greatest of all the sufferings I endure is revealed every time I look in the mirror. My presence now brings the greatest displeasure to the eyes. I, Ophelia, have grown old.

I have become a relic of a by-gone age, and as such, no one ever visits unless you count the therapy cats that lounge about. They are litter trained, but they shed and keep me awake at night with their nocturnal mischief; they lap from the toilet bowl, knock the books from my bedside table, and yowl at the window. And sometimes, when I am alone, they gather at the foot of my bed and converse in that sly, counterfeit way of theirs of things that I have spent the last 400 years trying to forget.

If it were not for my beloved night nurse, Verona, my life as it is, would be completely and utterly joyless. Though she refuses to acknowledge my noble heritage, she does grant me certain privileges. Verona is the only one who reads me stories when I can't sleep. She is gentle and kind and she never fails to come to my aid when I get hysterical. Whenever I press that little button or yell into the hollow depths of the night, she comes cussing down the hall, making a big thing about what an inconvenience I am. How I love those moments of reprieve. I make requests from the library—literature mostly, stories that Verona pretends to hate. She has a low opinion of what she calls "highbrow indulgences." And yet, more often than not, she indulges me. "I'm not supposed to be reading anybody bedtime stories," she says, handing me two Triazolam and a glass of water. "Next thing, you'll be asking for warm milk and cookies." But I am not completely at her mercy. I have managed to hoard a stash of pills from those late-night dramas. A simple matter of technique—slip sedative under tongue, sip water, swallow, raise hand to mouth, cough, and voila, another two pills in fist. Verona responds with a kind smile that shows off her white teeth. "All's well that ends well," she whispers.

I give thought to calling Verona now—she would make short work of getting me back to bed—but I have other plans. Tonight is the occasion of my final performance and with my bare feet cold on the tiled bathroom floor, it feels as if time is out of joint. Hamlet was indeed right on that account. And so I'll just have to be patient with this business with my bowels.

When relief finally does come, my insides gurgle, a trickle of pee, a spasm of bewildering pain, and the tension subsides. I use one hand to hold the roll and the other to tear along the perforated line. The toilet paper feels like burlap. I take a deep breath and haul myself up, but the moment I'm on my feet, my legs threaten to give out and I have no choice but to lower myself back down again. Perhaps it would have been better to have died young, I think, to have simply followed the script, to have climbed a willow *that grows aslant the brook*. But I can't be sure of anything anymore. The very ground has become unstable. *Tremors*, Verona calls them. She has a name and an explanation for everything. Accordingly, *osteoporosis*, *arthritis*, and *constipation*, are common, if not inevitable, conditions of one as aged as myself. "You live long enough," she says, "and the body breaks down and the mind, it loses its acuity."

I reach forward from where I am seated on the toilet and manage to get the door open, but my knickers are still around my ankles and I feel the heady, swirling approach of yet another one of my *age-related conditions*. I do my best to stay focussed, but when I spy the fat tabby lurking outside the bathroom door, the sweet bells jangle out of tune, time tumbles and spins, and all at once, I'm back in Stratford, the year 1616, a Saturday night in a flat above the Old Windmill Inn. The bard, William Shakespeare, slumped forward at his desk, his face pressed into the ink-smeared pages of his most recent play, a warm glass of ale in one hand, a quill in the other, and seven feral cats at his feet.

The whole tragic mess began with a broken pane of glass in William's study window. Seeking shelter from the incessant rain outside, the neighbourhood possums and squirrels found their way into his studio. As the days went by, the creatures' numbers increased and before long, they were nesting, rooting, and defecating willy-nilly. You can imagine the smell. William was struggling with the play *Titus Andronicus* at the time and, while he was troubled by the uninvited guests, it wasn't until he found himself brushing scat from the seat of his chair with the sleeve of his tunic that he decided that something had to be done. He had a hammer and a slat of pine in his hand when, as if on cue, the seven mangy cats scuttled one-by-one through the broken pane. Within moments, the possums and squirrels were surrounded, and then, in a fur-flying melee, the un-housebroken squatters were evicted. By the end of the day, even the mice that lived in the walls were gone. Compared to the previous intruders, the cats were prone to long spells of inactivity; they napped and seemed to be, if well fed, quite congenial company. And so, despite the chill in the air and his wife Anne's repeated pleas to administer repair to the broken glass, William simply wrapped his shoulders in a quilt and, when necessary, warmed his hands next to the flame of a candle.

The feral cats stayed, the window remained un-repaired, and, by the end of the week, they were all on a first-name basis.

Naming the cats was one thing, but before long, William could be heard taking advice and otherwise responding to suggestions the cats made regarding his script. He began to work late into the night and would often fall asleep at his desk. When Anne found William feeding them from a platter of bread, cheese, and sardines that she had prepared for his lunch, she gave him a piece of her mind. "It reeks in here," she said, glaring at the seven cats vying for position around her husband's ankles. "At least groom the damn things on occasion. Especially that one." She pointed at Thomas Dekker, a scraggly heavyweight who often came home from his late-night carousing in a matted and bloody mess. William's reply was defensive and slurred. "I'll have you know, dear wife, that these beasts, as unkempt as they may be, possess an uncanny talent for plot and twist." The foolishness of this claim was proof enough that the pint of ale in his hand was the product of more than one trip to the pub downstairs. Anne slammed her fist down on his desk, smudging a newly inked line. "The fool would rather cohabitate with mangy felines than inspire the affections of his wife," she hollered. Her parting words struck a chord of melancholy in the bard, the tone of which permeated the air of his derelict studio.

If there were deeper and more troubling issues at the heart of her grievances, the cats proved to be the final straw. A fortnight later, Anne moved her things to a nearby cottage where she took up the cultivation of orchids.

These remembrances, tainted as they are with the scent of urine and rosemary, alert me to the fact that I am in between. Ophelia of the stage and Ophelia trapped here on the toilet. I can feel the tug of it, as if my mind is being pulled in two. When I hear my own voice, agitated and wild, the tears burn down my cheeks and I try to rise. But then invisible arms embrace me. A moment later, a cool cloth on my forehead. "Shhh," Verona's familiar voice whispers, "you're just having another one of your episodes."

I take a breath but the hysteria still has me. "It takes imagination, luck, and some heavy detergents to get away with murder," I say. "But scrub as you may, like the conscience, the fingernails never come totally clean." I slump sideways against the bathroom wall, my rear still deposited in the toilet seat.

"There, there, you poor thing."

I feel myself being lifted; Verona's strong, reassuring arms guide me to bed.

"I recommend soaking in vinegar," I add. "The clothes you burn. The cats you toss in a sack with a heavy stone, condemn them to the bottom of a brook."

Verona's bosom brushes across my face as she tucks me in. When she's done, she gently touches my cheek. "You're so pale," she says. I feel the trauma recede back down into my spastic bowels. Another breath or two and I begin to calm down, but when I notice the syringe, a new wave of panic churns in my gut. I don't want to be—must not be—medicated tonight! When I open my mouth, all I can manage is more nonsense. Sleep, I tell myself, feign sleep, and all will be well. I hear Verona sigh. Her soft lips on my forehead.

Alas, the prick of the needle does not come. Verona's practical white shoes squeak as she lumbers towards the door. She turns out the light. "Sweet dreams," I hear her say. I wait for the familiar click of the lock before I struggle to free myself from the confines of the tightly tucked blankets. It's okay now. I see that my suitcase is still there, its lime-green handle just visible from under the bed. Packed as it was earlier that day when I managed to steal a moment between my morning Metrazol-induced seizure and my afternoon Gestalt group. I reach forward and open the bedside drawer in the night-stand. My makeup bag is there, my jewelry, my dress, now all I have to do is remember my lines.

'Tis evident that my wits should be as mortal as an old man's life, which is to say, I know how crazy my story sounds—to suggest that the seven cats had anything to do with it—the new play or the demise of their marriage. But once, in a drunken stupor, William credited the felines with the authorship of his darkest work. "The sonnets and the comedies were mine," he said, stroking the ringed tail of the one he called George Peele. "But the cats are responsible for all the violent dramas."

Though I bore witness to these developments from offstage, it was evident that Anne's departure and the persuasive methods of the seven cats were taking their toll on William. He was being bullied and manipulated. The one with the white feet, the big tabby, Christopher Marlowe, was of the foulest of tempers and had taken to using William's bottom drawer as a litter box. Henry Neville, a smoky grey, often swiped at William's ankles when he passed and the lot of them would gather on his desk and assume a posture of attack whenever William tried to enforce his will upon them. As the interlopers grew lazy and fat on pub fare and alcohol, William's handwriting grew shaky and the plots of his plays grew more sinister.

I loathed the cats, and yet, I owed one of them my life.

I was little more than an idea at the time, a minor character in a yet to be named work-in-progress. Young, underestimated, not fully written, and yet somehow I saw how it was going—the king poisoned, his brother taking the throne, and my betrothed's feigned lunacy. What I first thought were voices rattling about in my head, I eventually recognized as the creative ponderings of my authors. I could hear them conspiring, fragmented discussions that paired my name with some kind of a mental affliction. It eventually became clear that they were manufacturing what was to be my terrible and tragic demise. To make matters worse, they spoke of my fate as if it were an appetizer they had selected from a menu. I was, quite simply, overwhelmed by a sense of indignation. And while William and the cats gathered at the desk to ink this latest development, I caught hold of a tail as it swung lazily across the page. Act IV, scene VII.

"Unacceptable," I hollered as I rose from the script.

My presence shocked William to his feet so abruptly that he overturned the chair he was sitting in. Christopher Marlowe leapt onto the bureau, Ben Jonson retreated between William's legs, Thomas Dekker crouched low under the desk, Edward de Vere swatted at my hand, reminding me that I still had hold of his mottled tail. John Fletcher and George Peele peered out from behind the overturned chair as William, quill in hand, ventured a step closer. "Ophelia?" He said my name like a question.

"The one and only," I replied.

A moment passed, during which the cats surrounded me and proceeded to sniff at my feet as if I were a filet of dried carp.

"—A trick of smoke and mirrors," William speculated out loud.

When he poked me with the pointy end of his quill, I snatched the thing from his grasp and threw it to the floor.

"Witchcraft or some other ungodly hocus-pocus," he added.

I had the forces of self-preservation on my side, which I was determined to prove was greater than the passivity of my fictional temperament. "I am a noblewoman," I said. "And there is no magic of any sort to it. I am here in protest."

"In protest of what exactly?"

"I will not be exterminated or otherwise have my character rendered so insignificantly."

William reached for his glass and downed the rest of his ale. "I sympathize," he said, wiping at his beard. "But your heart is already pledged to Hamlet. And your mind, well, it is already touched." He then looked over at the seven cats. "The truth is," he added, "I am, like you, just a pawn in this tale of woe."

William's breath was sour, his tongue pale and slightly blue. "Then your play is doomed," I said with as much conviction as I could muster. "I'm not going back."

William righted his chair and took a seat. "Nothing surprises me since Macbeth," he said. "That's when things started to get out of hand. Those Weird Sisters…"

The phenomenon of my presence was eventually categorized as something akin to a tenacious hallucination, something to be tolerated like the damn cats and the weather coming in the broken window.

From where I was sitting defiantly in the corner, it didn't take long to figure out that William's own life was as messed up as the script I had escaped from. The cats were in control. He moped about like a defeated man, barely making an effort to avoid trodding on the garbage strewn about the room. I decided then and there that if I was going to get the script revised, I'd have to gain William's favour. And while I considered such things well below my station, I swept the floor, organized his stationery, scrubbed the ink stains from his desktop, and drew the curtains to let more light into the room. William seemed pleased with my efforts. "Thank you," he said with a smile. But when his eyes fell on the cats, who were in private conference by the stove, a look of despondency returned to his face. "Anne was right about them. I fear it's too late now for all of us."

When I told him I would help him get his wife back, he looked me squarely in the eye. "Impossible" he said. "When that woman makes up her mind..."

"It's simple," I said. "Take a bath and—" I pointed at his desk. "Iambic pentameter, rhyming couplets—you are a poet, William— write her a poem." I slid a fresh sheet of parchment in front of him and placed the quill in his hand.

"Very well," he said, staring down at the blank page. "But how to begin?"

I was shaking my head at this point. The man may have been a genius, but he was a fool. "The thought of her warms your heart," I offered. "Compare her to a summer's day."

"That's good," he said, as he reached for the ink, but then he looked up at me with a forlorn look in his eye. "Lovely and temperate she is not," he whispered. "And since she left, all my words are short and lame of breath and stumble."

"Get thee to a bathroom and acquaint yourself with a bar of soap," I said in frustration. "If need be, I will write her on your behalf."

We sealed the agreement with a handshake. But our plan never did come to fruition because three days later, William was dead.

I had been out buying orchids from Anne, commissioned as I was to make the purchase and return with a report on her countenance. I selected three exquisite specimens: a Catasetum, a Laelia, and a Lady's Slipper. "Keep them clear of direct sunlight and drafts of cold air," she said. "If the leaves go dark, they need more light and if they take on a reddish hue, they need less." We then exchanged comments regarding the weather and I took note of her complexion. Compared to William's pale skin and bloodshot eyes, she seemed well enough, but it was obvious she was burdened by a degree of sadness and heartbreak. I slipped an envelope containing several pages of verse into her mailbox when I departed.

It was late afternoon and a cool drizzle had turned the streets to muck. I shivered when I opened the studio door. It was damp and dim and the stove had gone cold. I hurried past the cats, who were gathered in one of their conspiratorial huddles on the sofa and rekindled the fire. I then busied myself with the flowers, arranging them just so on a shelf, which I determined was far enough away from the chilly window. I confess I fussed with the orchids for quite some time before I even noticed that William was at his desk. His body was slouched forward, a glass of ale in his left hand. At first, I thought he was drunk, passed out as I had found him once or twice before, but when I lit a lantern, I saw the knife protruding from his back. I felt my own breath catch in my lungs. It wasn't until I got to his side that I saw the gaping wound of his open mouth, his usually well-manicured beard—a mess of coagulated blood, saliva, and ink.

Even if William did call for help, no one would have heard him because the cats had, at some point in the melee, removed his tongue, which, for your information, is where the adage originated. The horrible thing was lying on his desk, still damp with spit. When I looked back over at the cats, one of them had a quill in its paws. Perhaps I should have made haste to the nunnery, but a page turned, the curtain closed, and all went black.

And that, I suppose, is how I ended up here in this madhouse— a raving lunatic, a hysterical nutter, an actress without a play.

Can I measure these 400-odd years of limbo against the drowning that I have thwarted? Does it matter that Shakespeare's compositions were co-written by a pack of flea-bitten alley cats? Does it matter that he was murdered? These questions have only inspired an incision made strategically above my hairline, monthly electric charges arcing through my pulse, and the daily intake of sedatives chased with a cup of tap water. Am I sane? I am only certain that I am, no matter what they do to me, still alive—

Here, in this dressing room, I stare at my reflection in the mirror. I push back against the tears and apply the foundation. I then sweep a brushstroke of blush up and outward to my hairline on both cheeks. I blend three layers of blue eyeshadow onto each eyelid. The eyeliner is trickier with my shaky hands, but I manage a decent line. I curl my eyelashes and apply mascara. My thin lips I trace with a tube of lipstick. The diamond earrings require a bit of force, but I get them through my overgrown lobes. The pearls rest heavy against my throat. By the time I am back in bed, it is 3 a.m., but I am ready.

I place the book on the nightstand, shift my body to the edge of the mattress, and pull the suitcase out from under the bed. Despite the restraints, the bars on the window, the lock on the door, I am finally going home, to Denmark, to fulfill my literary duty.

I drink and, this time for real, gulp back my lethal stash of pills like a good patient. I squeeze the little red button activating the signal at the nurse's station. I hear Verona's slow shuffle down the hall.

Her breath is heavy when she enters the room. When she gets to my bed, she stands there a moment looking down at me with a look of astonishment. "What have you gotten up to?" she asks. "You got a date tonight?"

"Do I look pretty?" I ask her.

She purses her lips, pauses, and gives me a nod.

I hold back the nonsense dancing in my head—*by his cockle hat and staff, and his sandal shoon...* "Verona," I whisper. "I can't sleep."

She shakes her head and sighs, and I smile as she relaxes her considerable bulk into the chair.

"What do we have here?" Verona says. She holds the book to the light, examines its twisted spine, the damp, swollen pages.

"It's Shakespeare," I answer. "Read me the part where Ophelia drowns."

ACKNOWLEDGEMENTS

First and foremost I am indebted to my partner Rain Bone, whose ongoing support and quiet understanding are so deeply appreciated.

A warm thank you to the literary journals that published some of the stories in this collection along the way. Thanks to the team at Enfield & Wizenty for bringing my second book to life, and to Lee Kvern, whose editorial feedback was crucial.

I am also grateful to the university of Guelph MFA program, Undercurrents, Naoko Kumagi, and the literary support of Lisa McLean, Kasia Jaronjek, Bob Young, Luke Hill, and Shane Neilson.

Some stories in this collection (or versions of them) have been previously published as follows: "Foreword" as "An Open Love Letter" at www.paperplates.com Vol.6 No.2; "Flotsam and Jetsam" in *Paperplates*, vol 6 no. 4, "Silence" in *Descant*, issue 145; "Aberrations" as "Details" in *Exile* vol. 27 issue 2; "Still Life with Rotten Fruit" in *Other Voices*, vol. 20, no. 1; "Red" in *Pottersfield Portfolio*, volume 23 no. 2; and "Hungry Ghosts" as "A Crack in Everything" in PRISM *International* issue 42:3.